Moon
and the
Imp

A DREAM FANTASY FOR DREAMERS

JO KEMRICH

About the author

Author, Jo Kemrich, lives in the West Country. After working as a solicitor and legal writer for many years, Jo retired to concentrate on writing fiction of another sort. *"It's just pleasure. I put the characters on page one; they get on with writing the story they want to be in. I sit back and let them do it. What could be easier? Well, quite a lot of things really; now, brain surgery for example ......"*

For Jackie

Itinerary:

So it begins   ix

An introduction   xi

Summer morning   xiii

Chapter 1: Moon has a bad night   1

Chapter 2: Sun misses a friend and several meals   8

Chapter 3: More trouble for Moon   16

Chapter 4: Earth sleeps on and on and on…   31

Chapter 5: Advice from far away   35

Chapter 6: Sun at home   40

Chapter 7: Martian dream   49

Chapter 8: Adventures and friendship   60

Chapter 9: Friends, food and familiar things   90

Chapter 10: Bowls and practical jokes   104

Chapter 11: Partings   115

Summer afternoon   127

So it begins

Trouble; Ah! How it spreads, sticking to all it touches.

Its immediate family were gathered to see it leave, or more accurately, to make sure it was really going and not playing another painful practical joke. Unknown to it, a special Celebration Leaving party was being arranged for later that evening with just a few relatives and friends attending, a fine spread of food and plenty of bubbly drink.

Following established etiquette on these occasions, the father made an attempt at the usual farewell speech. He didn't find this easy - there wasn't much that was nice to say - and he stumbled awkwardly through his few formal words of parting:

"Well, my dear firstborn, it's my pleasure … No, I should say, my solemn duty, to send you on your way and wish you well through the next few years wherever fate takes you and whoever you may meet.

Remember, if you can: be kind to others; kinder than you've been to your family. Value those who offer friendship. (At this point he might have added *"Sadly you haven't valued any of us"* but he had no wish to be unkind).

"As to your return, you are well aware of our Rules. We look forward to seeing you once you mature into a responsible being. When (and if) you achieve this, I shall be pleased to invite you home. Do not return before then.

On behalf of us all, I wish you farewell."

The rest of the family drifted away expecting nothing more to interest them - and there was a feast to prepare.

It had stayed silent while its father made this rather cold speech. Whether or not it had taken any notice is uncertain – probably not - but now, with head on one side and a slight quivering of anticipation, it was listening for some new sound.

And that sound came. A loud scream from the family kitchen, then a great crash, more voices screaming and a strong smell of burning food.

Its mother, jostled by the two identical sisters, appeared, choking, at the kitchen doorway followed by clouds of smoke and steam. All three were red-faced but otherwise covered entirely in something that looked like hot, white custard, two were in tears, the mother furiously shaking a fist.

Just visible through the half open door, some thick substance was dripping slowly from the kitchen ceiling.

It giggled, tried to change this into a cough, failed and burst into uncontrollable squeaky laughter.

"If that's your doing, whatever it is, and another of your disgraceful pranks at your poor mother's expense, then we shall all be glad to see you leave! Even one more night under my roof would be …"

But its father's words were wasted. The young trouble maker had vanished as is the magical way of its kind. Where had it gone? Don't ask, just be grateful it hasn't called at your house while you were out!

Or perhaps it has.

By way of footnote, you may like to know that the Celebration Leaving party went very well. The family's relief at not having to worry about any more tricks being played on them quite made up for having to eat out and the father gave a warm and friendly speech that pleased and cheered everyone present, including himself.

It was, however, some long time before the kitchen was usable again and the decorators' bills were substantial.

An Introduction

All great deeds start from little thoughts. So must we dream or adventures could never be.

Some time ago, I can't recall quite when, there came into existence beings that, for convenience, we shall refer to as imps.

This was not their proper name which was a good deal longer and quite difficult to spell even in the language used in those times. But it will serve for the purposes of this (nearly true) little story in which one imp played a leading part, and on the way both taught and learned some valuable lessons on such varied subjects as the importance of being kind to others, looking where you are going when you travel and how to play a game of Bowls.

We think of imps today (if we think of them at all in these selfish times) as small troublesome creatures that are best avoided for fear of what they might do to us, like knotting our shoelaces together or pouring hot water on the cat.

This is only partly true; in their early lives they tend to be spiteful and fond of practical jokes of the meanest sort, choosing to attach themselves to individuals and to make their lives as miserable as possible.

In these cases, the individual is said to be imp ridden. The only cure being patience and the hourly application of a strong sense of humour.

Naturally this behaviour has got them a well-deserved bad press. However, many (but by no means all) imps eventually grow up to become quite decent citizens of the Universe and the most dependable of friends.

As to their appearance, imps vary in size according to the degree of trouble they are making at any one time. The more trouble, the smaller, which is unfortunate as a small imp is hard to locate and, if you are trying to find the source of your annoyances, you need a clear and substantial target to aim for.

Their colour varies. It is most often black but imps can change this to match their background and, for shape and detail, I can only say they have a lot in common with ants, but without so many legs and antennae. Although of course imps are a lot larger than even the biggest ant and ants have no ears, or if they do, their ears don't stick out, so they may as well not have them at all.

So much for facts. I can add just one further piece of information:

It is rumoured that imps have an unusual - but not unique - way of raising their young:

Apparently, parent imps send their offspring out alone into the Universe when they become the equivalent of teenagers. Effectively they are abandoned and allowed (even sometimes encouraged) to misbehave in society for the next few decades and to do whatever impish things they choose in that time.

It's also said they are allowed to return home only after they have matured past their period of impish nuisance. Whether or not this is so, I can't say.

Now you know all I can tell of imps in general, for the story that follows concerns one particular imp which may or may not be typical of its kind.

The rest of the characters in this fairly (or nearly) accurate historical record will be well known to you as they are always around and about.

Although often ignored by us on a day-by-day basis, they exercise a surprising amount of control over our lives and it's as well to respect them and their considerable powers at all times, not merely when we need their help.

Summer morning

In dreams or in waking, where does truth lie?

The sun's warmth seemed to increase strongly; its light streamed through the leaves above her; she sat, then laid back in the deep orchard grass and half closed her eyes. Sounds of some family argument drifted in and out of hearing; it was comforting to lie here alone in the orchard; away from the others for a while at least.

One voice rose above the rest, demanding dominance - Jessica, of course - she always had to win.

"Well, I want to stay here for the rest of the day and I'm going to, whatever the rest of you ..."

The words faded as if their speaker moved further away, or perhaps the wind was rising, nature taking over, pushing the intrusive alien noises back wherever they belonged, re-establishing the proper order; natural things first, last and always; sun, the glorious cherry trees, wind in their beautiful, shapely, dark green leaves, birdsong, insects – how they buzzed in the great masses of spring blossom!

A very round moon was riding high in a bright blue sky dotted and streaked with white clouds, the highest of them thin and drawn out as if by quick brush strokes indicating a brisk wind at that high level. Lower down little cauliflowers sailed sedately along, each one a surprisingly perfect portrayal of something. - Here an aged woman in an old-fashioned bonnet, there a whale being chased by a flock of sheep …

She closed her eyes, shutting out one sense to allow full appreciation of others: the rich flowery smell, wind sweeping across the grass, ever louder insect sounds. And, very quietly at first, voices again, but this time, unfamiliar.

She couldn't make out what was being said but it didn't matter – this was a conversation that melted into nature's background, comfortingly accepting her presence and her right to be there.

Then words came more clearly and just a little louder as if from strong voices spoken a long way off.

"It never seems right for Moon to be out on a sunny day. The two of them ought to stick to their proper times. Except of course when they eat cherries and cauliflowers before a Planetary Bowls match."

Somewhat astonished by such rubbish, and thinking her hearing might have let her down, she struggled against sleep, turning the words around in her mind and yet making ever less sense of them.

Now a different voice, higher, almost squeaky:

"I shall be writing new rules soon, there has to be an end to players setting light to each other so often. Rule number one will ban poke bonnets and whales will have to keep sheep under control if they want to stay in the First Team."

She heard no more and, if the distant conversation continued that day, she did not remember it, for sleep places most dreams beyond waking reach (and we may all be glad of that). Yet every now and again in later years, she heard or thought she heard the same voices speaking of mystifying matters as if they wanted her to hear them and to understand.

Chapter 1

Moon has a bad night

For a picnic on Summer's green riverbank, give me friends and Sun's bright day but I had rather by far walk the starry night alone save for Moon to show my way. Then what adventures may follow!

It was the end of a glorious day: Sun had been in fine form, leaving her daughter, Earth - and everyone else within her long reach - warm, cheered and comforted.

Having painted the evening sky in soft pinks and greens, with nothing in the Universe to worry her, she was looking forward to dinner (followed by a little extra supper or two) before peaceful and well-earned sleep.

Moon on the other hand was just getting up and struggling with his rather awkward pyjamas (which of course had no legs or arms and were therefore very confusing, especially if, like Moon, you were a circular person).

I'm sorry to say that on this particular evening he had quite a fight with his uncooperative bedwear and this was followed by an equally difficult time with his new all-in-one night time suit which he had chosen to wear for that night's work. At his first attempt he found he had this on inside out. Next, that it was upside down so that he couldn't see at all.

By this time, he had become quite upset and very red in his usually cheerful creamy coloured face.

This was not a good beginning to Moon's night and I can't help but think he would have avoided a lot of his subsequent hardships if his pyjamas, or whatever power controlled them, had been better behaved at the start of it.

Just why Moon's nightwear had been so troublesome and why he was uncharacteristically so irritable, is a mystery that may become clear later (or it may not).

At this point you need to know that Moon lived in an inside out sort of way.

Getting up when night came was as normal to him as the habit of rising at the start of the day was natural to Sun. And, quite naturally for him, Moon woke up, dressed himself (in properly circular clothes) and had his breakfast when the rest of the world was enjoying a bedtime drink or getting thrown out of the pub.

Now, although Sun and Moon were very great friends (in fact they were as closely related as, say, humans are to their grandmothers) and had already been through several adventures together, Moon was just a little envious of Sun's amazing powers, like melting ice caps and hatching birds' eggs.

This wasn't helped by the fact that Sun was inclined to be just a trifle overbearing and to say rather boastful things of the sort that are better not said, except under one's breath for one's hearing alone.

On the other hand, Sun was sometimes a bit irritated with herself that, for his part, Moon could do a lot of very special and important things that Sun could not do, like frightening people on lonely roads at midnight and playing with Earth's oceans by making them rise and fall in a most entertaining fashion.

It was a source of great amusement for Moon to see Sun attempting, and failing, to perform some of Moon's own special actions when she mistakenly thought no-one was looking. But their friendship was far too deep to be affected by such little jealousies.

Now, on this day we are talking about, Moon was still grumpy as he hadn't enjoyed his breakfast very much. His tea had been cold, his toast decided to burn so he had to eat marmalade without anything to help it go down and, worse still, there was no milk. And we all know how upsetting that can be.

Being irritable when he climbed into the heavens to start his nightly journey, for no good reason he was uncharacteristically upset to find that Sun had been happily painting a wonderful sky by way of saying goodnight to everybody.

In his heart Moon knew, of course, that Sun's painting was quite beautiful, because all her artwork is. But, as he couldn't paint in colours himself and because he felt grumpy anyway, he said in quite a loud voice (which fortunately no-one of importance heard as everyone else was asleep, except a few stars who picked up the waves of Moon's speech but were too far off to matter):

"What a poor sky! Those colours don't look right at all, who ever heard of pink and green for a sky picture?"

Moon went on in this way, criticising and complaining until he was quite hoarse with all the effort of talking to himself. Just as one might expect of someone who has had only one cup of tea since getting up and that one cold.

He was still muttering about the painted evening sky long after Sun had quietly and gently wiped it away.

That was just the start of a night that Moon did not enjoy one bit.

Things went from bad to worse.

When Sun's delightful picture had vanished with the night, Moon set about illuminating Earth himself. But try as he did, for some mysterious reason that we may discover later, the best light he could manage was just a weak glow. This did very little to help either people or animals find their way about on Earth's surface and nothing at all to make plants grow (which is another of Sun's special accomplishments).

Naturally moonlight is never sufficient to help grow trees and grass, or even nasty things like brussels sprouts. However, it can light things up at night quite well enough to show people their way home and help animals get their food and avoid things that threaten them.

Moon felt even more aggrieved by the failure of his hard work. Especially since he kept thinking of how Sun effortlessly brought daylight and good cheer wherever and whenever she went whilst his own efforts were generally not much appreciated, as most of the time people were asleep when Moon was sailing the sky and on the top of his form.

Of course, there were those who were often very appreciative of moonlight, like smugglers hauling barrels of rum up the beach and grave robbers busy with their excavations. All of whom would have been put out of a useful job if Sun had suddenly decided to work a double shift day and night.

But on this particular night, with an unexpected shortage of moonlight, the smugglers and their nocturnal colleagues (who were tripping over things and cursing the dark) were most annoyed to be falling into long, narrow holes in churchyards or accidently running into customs and excisemen on the cliffs.

Taken altogether, this left hardly anyone at all to say nice things about poor Moon.

By now he was feeling quite wretched, especially as he is one of those beings that need people to think well of them and, more importantly, to say as much in his hearing.

Perhaps just because he was in a low frame of mind, he began to think even less well of himself and ever more aggrieved about his friend, Sun.

As we all know, it is very easy to fall into that sort of trap; one thing goes wrong and it isn't very long before our whole world gets somehow out of tune. We spill the milk which for some unaccountable reason leaves the jug before it was asked to, then promptly drop a cup, find our shirts are on back to front and finally, the postman brings us a bill instead of that nice parcel we expected from a favourite great aunt.

On such occasions it's tempting to go back to bed and try again tomorrow. But this wasn't a practical solution for Moon because going to bed at night would never have occurred to him and in any case, if he went back home, he had nothing very special in his food cupboards to cheer him up.

That thought was more depressing than almost everything else that had been going wrong for him. So he floundered on through his unhappy night.

Indeed, he floundered for such a long time and in such mounting despair that, quite without realising it, he was still high in the sky long after Sun had risen.

Not only had she risen but Sun had painted a nice red and gold dawn, tidily rubbed it out again and was now well on her way to her High Point. - That being the time when she generally had a substantial lunch followed by a quiet doze and a light snack of assorted sandwiches with a slice or more of cake and a few pots of refreshing tea.

When Moon realised his situation, he was quite alarmed as, being someone of fixed and dependable habits, he didn't at all like finding himself in unexpected places at the right time or expected places at wrong times.

Also, he always felt more than a little uncomfortable if he was still up and about when Sun was shining so very hard.

As I have said, Moon and Sun were the greatest of friends but in Sun's very brightest light (around lunchtime on a Summer's day for example) Moon would look down at himself (he could roll his eyes about in a most surprising way to view his own round person) and it seemed to him on these worrying occasions that he looked quite transparent and unwell.

This was very worrying for Moon who, at the best of times, was inclined to think he wasn't eating enough.

Perhaps unfortunately for them both, just at this time of her busy day, Sun was rather distracted by the planning of several forthcoming meals with the result that she failed to notice Moon sitting there in the sky almost beside her. Also of course she was busy with her daily tasks of illuminating Earth and anything else that might need her attention.

As we all know, even if you expect to see him, you have to look quite hard to spot Moon on those forgetful occasions when he is wandering about and looking rather transparent in a bright blue mid-day sky. You might almost think it isn't Moon at all but one of his long departed ghostly ancestors who has just popped in to see how much things have changed so that it can go back home to complain comfortably to its friends about what a mess the Modern Universe is getting itself into.

Whatever the reasons, the fact is that on that eventful day Sun did not see Moon but Moon certainly saw Sun who was so bright just then she could hardly have been missed even if one had one's eyes closed.

Fate being what she is, of course, sad Moon quite wrongly thought that the naturally carefree Sun was unkindly ignoring him.

Coming on top of his earlier troubles, thinking his old and very dear friend had cast him off was too much for Moon to bear so he rolled quietly away, back to his rather unwelcoming home where he rolled into his rocking chair and reflected on what he should do.

☽ ☺ ☾

Now deciding on anything concerning one's future is not a task to be approached with a heavy heart or when you have run out of milk for your tea. It's an occasion to be bright and positive. But Moon wasn't feeling either cheerful or logical at that moment and a little imp either inside, or at least very near to him, was saying:

> *"Nobody loves you Moon. You have to go away, find some new and lonely place to live where you can't be found even if anyone wanted to, which naturally they don't."*

Well, that was nonsense of course because Moon is greatly loved by just about everyone in Sun's Solar System, except a few celestial oddments who live so far off that they don't know about him and therefore don't count.

But, as you may have guessed, the troublesome little imp was to get its way. Otherwise this almost entirely true story, in which only some names and a few unimportant trifling details have been changed to protect your author against horrid law suits, would have been a very short tale indeed and, whilst interesting, possibly just a bit less exciting.

Chapter 2

Sun misses a friend and several meals

***Tales set free our minds and warm our hearts. Where
would we be but for good stories to tell of hardships
suffered and better times that followed?***

In many ways Sun and Moon are very different – well, you only
have to look at them to see that much - but it would be misleading
to describe them as opposites.

They are both cheerful and friendly at heart and they both
enjoy many of the same things (like grilled bacon with fried
potatoes and plenty of mushrooms with more toast to follow and
nice new suits of round clothes to keep in their equally nice round
wardrobes).

I should also mention, in case you haven't noticed this already,
that both friends are very fond of pretty much every sort of good
food for which they always have some spare room, even just after
they have finished a meal. In fact some of their happiest times are
spent sitting around a well loaded dining table along with a few
of their planetary family all of whom share the same liking for
something tasty and plenty of it. They are, after all, all very round
and all of them do their best to stay that way at all times.

But, despite their many similarities, there is one great difference
between the two friends; Sun is a day person, Moon is not.

If Sun stays up too late, she quickly feels uneasy about the
dark. She starts to have concerns about what might be lurking
under her circular bed and wonders if it would be best to keep the
light on all night.

Also nights are full of odd noises which Sun's imagination turns into the sound of ghosts trying the front door handle or something slimy coming down the chimney when in fact it is probably just the central heating trying to soothe Sun while she has her post-supper supper.

But Moon, on the other hand, likes the dark and has no fears of it at all. That is except when he encounters ghostly beings at his front door or green slime in the fireplace. On these occasions he has to roll speedily into his kitchen and fortify himself with a cup of strong tea and a few toasted sandwiches followed by a cake or two.

And Sun, as her name suggests, has a very sunny disposition whilst Moon is a more serious person, quite ready to chuckle when it is proper to do so but at times rather disturbed and embarrassed by Sun's habit of publicly bursting into peals of golden laughter at any moment and often with no obvious reason.

Moon is very careful to do everything in the correct way and not to upset anyone that he does not know very well. But Sun doesn't much care what other people think of her and, as a result, is liked all the more for it.

In contrast poor Moon is sometimes thought to be a bit of a killjoy. This is most unfair, but people do rather avoid sitting or standing next to him at the annual Solar System Party in case they cannot roll away when the conversation flags and perhaps not even get to the table which holds the circular coffee machine and all the good things to eat which are, after all, the main attractions at those sorts of gatherings.

So you will understand how it was that, on the day we are talking about, light-hearted Sun, having busied herself painting a glorious cloud scene in purples and yellows (with not a hint of rain), was unconcernedly beaming down on daughter Earth while, in contrast, Moon was feeling thoroughly unhappy.

Free of all care Sun was happily planning a nice hot lunch to be followed later by an afternoon tea with various sandwiches and a fine chocolate cake, whilst not realising either that Moon was having a rotten day, or even that he was sitting in the summer sky beside her when he ought properly to have been gently snoring in his round bed after his usual early morning post-supper supper.

However, Moon was never out of Sun's kindly thoughts for very long. When the time came for the day to draw to a close, she decided to look in on her friend before she had a little post-supper supper of her own and went to bed.

Now one might think this part of our (mostly true) story cannot be right because Sun could not possibly go wandering off course in this way. Surely people would notice and make a big fuss by writing to newspapers or demonstrating with placards saying rude things about what the government was up to.

But Sun is always careful (unless she forgets) not to shine herself about the place when she pops out to visit someone or to take a peek at something special, like a new pastry shop.

That's how Sun's occasional off course wanderings go unnoticed by people here on Earth. Although Earth herself naturally knows all about them, unless she is sleeping - and she does do a great deal of that.

Seeking her friend, Sun called in to Moon's modest little home. Well, it's very modest and little compared with Sun's great golden hall but of course a whole lot larger than anything we are used to here on Earth because Moon is a whole lot bigger than any of us.

Now, you will always know when Moon is nearby. If he isn't making a noise like someone losing patience with his pyjamas or slipping in a slimy fireplace, then you may be sure there will be some lovely cooking smell of a roasting dinner or a tasty toast-and-something by way of a preliminary snack.

But, as Sun reached his doorway and called out to her friend, she could smell nothing and hear no sound. And, when she opened the door itself (without troubling to knock as Sun never bothered with such trifling etiquette, despite a couple of recent embarrassing incidents when a preliminary tap on a door might have saved a friendship), she saw only an empty room.

Well, it was empty of Moon although a bit untidy having a discarded marmalade pot and a suit of circular pyjamas on the floor.

A quantity of washing up awaited attention in the sink, including several empty milk bottles and half a cup of very cold milkless tea. There were also several smart creamy coloured and red striped pyjama buttons scattered about the place which puzzled Sun more than anything apart from her friend's disappearance.

This is a convenient moment to describe Moon's home which is luxurious but quite simple:

Apart from the very handsome guest suite a short distance away, it consists of just three main rooms. If you had looked down on them from above, they would have shown the pattern of a clover leaf. The smallest room is Moon's circular bathroom. The cream coloured kitchen is the largest room by far with plenty of cooking equipment and a fine round glass dining table which frequently entertains large numbers of its owners' friends. Lastly the circular bedroom has a great picture window, pale blue walls and a dark blue ceiling decorated with numerous silvery stars.

The circular furniture includes a number of useful cupboards. These are mainly for storing food. Most were largely empty at this time. First because food does not have a chance to go stale once it finds its way into Moon's establishment. Secondly, although Sun did not yet know this, most of the food that should have been there was at that very moment whizzing through space and, as we shall see, getting somewhat spoiled in its travels.

With only three rooms and some near empty cupboards to search it did not take long for Sun to check that Moon wasn't playing one of his practical jokes by hiding somewhere, just waiting to roll out of a cupboard with a loud squeal to surprise his visitor and make her laugh before they sat down to a comfortable snack together.

Sun then moved on to see what the guest suite might have to tell and we may as well take the opportunity to get to know it now because it later became a comfortable home for an important character in this narrative and you will rightly expect full and accurate details of that character's accommodation.

Although Moon refers to it simply as his "guest room", it's

almost a complete home in itself, standing a short distance from the main residence and connected to it by a wide, smooth path that curves on its way under a high, transparent roof.

A large circular entrance door opens into the cheerful and welcoming sitting area with its green carpet and matching circular chairs.

The walls are a lighter shade of green, the ceiling Moon's favourite creamy colour. Light floods in through a long ribbon of windows which provide constantly changing views out into beautiful star-studded space. Dark green curtains draw easily across to provide privacy, or a sense of cosiness, if wanted.

Everything about this space is luxurious and soothing. There is a faint smell of newness, like a showroom car. The chairs feel weighty but roll easily at the lightest touch. Doors and windows open and close smoothly, silently in such a pleasing fashion that you wish to go on operating them just for the pleasure of it.

Here and there are brightly coloured pictures – all done by Sun and mostly proud portrait groups of members of her Solar System.

These have a curious tendency to change when no one is looking so that a group showing Mars with helmet and spear, Mercury looking as hot as ever and Pluto being cool might later on the same day include Moon. What is more, everyone may have moved about and spun around to show different views of themselves.

Some visitors enjoy this feature as soon as they notice it, some don't notice at all and others find it a little disconcerting but grow to like it. After all, why should pictures not change themselves? How boring not to!

There are two further doors, both circular of course. The first gives access to a neat white bathroom with bright polished silver fittings, soft towels and all you might hope to find as a guest – Moon likes to have visitors and wants them to be very comfortable.

The bathroom gives direct access to a guest bedroom which is just as luxurious. Here creamy white paintwork and a soft light blue carpet provide the setting for a large welcoming bed with a cover of darkest blue decorated with silver stars.

The ceiling appears to match the bedcover but it is in fact transparent so that, lying in bed, guests fall asleep gazing peacefully into the infinite and calming depths of space.

The second door from the sitting area leads into a surprisingly large kitchen.

This is no poor arrangement of cheap kettle, two dusty tea bags, nasty long-life milk and no teaspoon as you will find in your disappointing hotel room. Here, instead, are cooking and eating utensils and circular cupboards containing a range of food to satisfy any guest who might wake at some odd hour with a sudden desire for a snack and perhaps a pot or two of tea or coffee.

But of course there won't be much food here if Moon doesn't have any visitors because he doesn't believe in letting things get stale.

The walls and floor of this bright room are creamy white. A light green table and four comfortable dining chairs (in darker green) stand close to a large picture window that frames the ever-changing skyscape. Or is it really another of Sun's own pictures?

The kitchen smells faintly of coffee and baking bread – except on the odd occasions when Moon pops in to prepare and share a pre-breakfast breakfast with his guests. Then toast and grilled bacon are more likely to dominate the room.

By way of welcome for the arriving guest there is always a plateful of freshly made sandwiches and a fine chocolate cake (with an inviting knife to hand) standing in the centre of the green table and, most probably, an assortment of pastries. - Moon simply can't stop himself from cooking when he's at home.

Continuing her search, Sun examined these guest rooms but discovered nothing new. The place had an empty, almost abandoned feeling. It was clear to her that Moon hadn't been there for some time.

She turned to leave and, as she did, noticed that one of her own portrait groups originally showing herself with Mars, Saturn and Moon all looking happily at you out of the picture had altered.

Staring at her painting Sun realised it was changing even as she looked at it.

Saturn was no longer in the picture and tiny Pluto had taken her place. Then she saw Moon was no longer looking outward. Facing in the opposite direction he was travelling away into deeper space. Pluto was following him. Even as Sun watched, Moon seemed to have travelled a little further. Soon, she felt, he must disappear altogether.

This was all very strange and rather alarming. Sun concentrated her mind on Moon's disappearing image, sending what comfort she could in Moon's direction, wherever he might be. Then she went back to the main house to gather her thoughts.

As Moon was very much a being of fixed habit, Sun was quite at a loss to work out what had happened to him or where he might be. The changing picture only added to the mystery.

Copying him without knowing it, she settled down into Moon's circular rocking chair (which could be made to roll over and over right around the room and was a great aid to digestion for anyone that needed it) and, sat thus, Sun tried to think what could have happened and what she ought to do.

She sat so long that she fell asleep without having her usual dinner or suppers or even her goodnight cocoa and cakes.

Doctors advise us *"do not go to bed on an empty stomach"*. By which, of course, they mean *"don't go to bed with an empty stomach"*.

Poorly worded but good advice and, unsurprisingly, lacking so many meals, Sun's dreams on this occasion had nothing to do with Moon and everything to do with food. So we need not trouble ourselves about them on this occasion.

When Sun woke, she still had no ideas on the question of how to deal with an absent Moon beyond deciding to ask for help from her large family on the basis that several heads are several times better than one.

This foolish old saying, however, is of course untrue, as several heads talking nonsense instead of one just leads to a good deal more nonsense and nothing useful at the end of it. And so it proved in this case.

Now we must leave Sun to choose her helpers and gather them together (for all the use they are going to be) and follow poor, sad Moon wherever his troubled mind is taking him.

Chapter 3

More trouble for Moon

Friends may be found wherever you go; just remember to look.

If you are going to travel, it is always as well to have some idea of where you are going and how long you will be away. Once you have those two matters clear, the next step is to make a careful list of what you will need for your trip by way of things to eat and to wear and boring stuff like passports, spare socks and spending money.

But, in his troubled state of mind, Moon was incapable of making lists and his travel preparations on that day were, to say the least, inadequate.

If anyone had asked Moon when he awoke earlier that evening, what he expected to be doing during the night, he would have described his timetable something like this:

Enjoy a pot of tea with biscuits in bed, a nice warm bath and dressing leisurely in something loose fitting to allow space for meals. Then a good solid cooked breakfast (and you may imagine what that might include).

This pleasant start would be followed by a smooth and graceful orbit across the dark blue sky - with no upsetting events - and a good meal at each of the proper times. That is to say: elevenses, lunch, early morning tea, high tea, dinner (a most important event with several good round courses starting with soup and ending with a box of chocolates and coffee), morning supper, post-supper top up, bedtime cocoa with something nice on toast and a piece of fruit cake, plus a few extra cups of tea and maybe a sandwich or two in between formal meals to keep himself in proper round form.

Of course, along with good things to eat and drink, Moon would have expected to enjoy cheerful talk and, later, perhaps a game or two of Bowls with some of his many friends, especially Sun and Earth.

{About Bowls:

As the game plays quite an important role in our story, for those few who are unfamiliar with it, this is a convenient moment for a brief description.

Bowls (or more correctly Planetary Bowls), is a favourite pastime in the Solar System in which the players themselves act as the bowls, rolling around a large (by our standards, vast) green lawn, bumping into one another, roaring with uncontrolled laughter and playing practical jokes on anyone who happens to be carelessly looking elsewhere just at that moment.

One big problem with this otherwise very popular game was that Sun frequently became rather over-excited and careless with the result that she set light to the grass as she rolled about. At this, all the players became bright red and choked either from the resulting smoke or because they couldn't stop laughing at each other's singed clothing.

Sun wasn't the only one guilty of fire raising. By the time of the events in this story, matters had reached a stage where, apart from those players who were naturally gifted with flames of their own, almost everyone now carried boxes of matches and joyfully used them in the course of a match whenever they had the opportunity.

So now you know the basics of this very genteel sport. Details of the Bowls scoring system and the game's history and Rules will have to wait their turn until later as we must get back to

Moon and his problems.}

In the last twenty four hours, few of these expected pleasant things had in fact occurred for Moon and those that had happened were almost no pleasure at all, not even his first pot of tea.

Lost in an unhappy world that was quite beyond his experience, he had no idea where to go and hardly cared. His mind had become incapable of rational thought.

He knew, or thought that he knew, only that he was unwanted. So, it seemed to him, that he must leave.

As to what he might need to take with him, he was so overwhelmed by despair that he could give no sensible thought to that problem at all.

In short Moon was imp ridden but did not yet know it.

Travel can mean holidays, visiting friends or just exploring somewhere new. These are pleasant events to look forward to and preparing for them is part of the enjoyment.

We get our travel cases off the top of the wardrobe, rummage about for our swimwear, search for sunglasses we haven't seen since last summer and generally make as much fuss as possible over the business of getting ready to set out.

In fact some people enjoy these happy tasks so much that they don't bother to go away on their holiday at all. Preparing for it is enough for them. Once their packed cases are neatly set down by the front door, these happy tourists settle down into their favourite chairs and spend a fortnight watching television at very little cost to their bank balances and without any of the fuss one gets at airports. And, of course, unpacking neatly folded clean clothes is pure pleasure compared with all that washing and ironing.

On the other hand this pre-holiday fuss isn't always a pleasure.

If, when you are gathering everything together, you find your swimwear has gained an awkwardly placed hole and you sit on your sunglasses, you may feel the whole business just isn't worthwhile.

Moon liked both holidays and getting ready for them but on this occasion, for the first time ever, there would be nothing of pleasure in his journey. Still, cheerless as it was, packing had to be done.

To meet his travel needs, Moon owned two cases.

One was quite small and beautifully round. This he only used for going to grand events when he wanted to appear at his very best – like eclipses, visits by comets and especially the Perseid showers on Swift-Tuttle day. This little case was a birthday gift from Mother Earth which he had always felt was a bit too good for the rough and tumble of everyday cosmic travel.

His other case was a lot larger but a very awkward and unnatural shape (it was square with nothing round about it at all).

This one he used most of the time for storing spare cakes. Just now it was almost empty save for a rather boring Victoria sponge which had far too little jam in it and some almost uneatable home-made macaroons which one of his cousins, a moon called Miranda, (who was an astonishingly bad cook) had sent to him for his birthday last year.

{You may like to know that Kindly Miranda always sent Moon gifts of home cooked food on his birthday and, being a very truthful being, he found it extremely difficult to express appropriately enthusiastic thanks.

Of course he did his best and somehow managed to give the impression he was pleased with his presents. The inevitable consequence was that he received more of the same the following year, after year, after …

Whilst we are here, I mention that this poor-cook-cousin performed much the same duties for another planet as our dear Moon performs for Earth. She was however rather put upon by having a very large and grasping family, too numerous for most people to count or, indeed, to find names for.

We may meet Miranda again later in our travels and on the other hand, we may not, so please don't hold your breath or you may go quite purple waiting to learn more and your author does not want that responsibility.}

Moon got on with his depressing task.

Apart from not being circular, which was very awkward, and not quite empty - which was quickly resolved, his big case could accommodate most of what Moon chose to take with him.

He was able to pack into it much of his store of food (which was rather small and uninteresting just at that moment) together with a few clothes, including his second-best pyjamas (that is the ones that still had a few buttons attached).

He also added some oddments that he grabbed almost randomly and with little considered thought.

These included his favourite picture of Sun wearing her usual big smile, his toothbrush and various other items that one may expect to find in a bathroom but which we need not name just now.

In his smart little round case he packed some more useful items, including a portable stove and a frying pan but these were of no subsequent use as he forgot both case and contents entirely, leaving them in the bottom of his circular wardrobe for Sun to discover later in her hunt for clues as to where her friend had gone.

Instead he mistakenly took with him a similar sized and equally round box labelled (had he troubled to read it):

"Christmas presents to be given next year".

Which was a polite and inoffensive way of writing:

"Useless items people gave me this year that I must pass on to someone else when I get the chance".

So our sad hero left his dear old home, where he had lived for quite a lot of years - more in fact than I dare name as he is, after all, a moon and therefore very old by human reckoning although quite young by Universe standards.

He was setting out on an unplanned and unwelcome journey without thinking what direction to take and wholly unaware of what was in store for him.

Indeed, even if he had thought about it, in his present state of mind, he could hardly have planned any route as he had no idea what he was doing, or why he was doing it, let alone where his travels would take him.

His little imp now had Moon completely under its spell and matters were going to stay that way for quite a long time to come.

However long journeys may be, they generally start in familiar surroundings before they ease into new and, hopefully exciting, places.

Moon's travel was at first a wandering affair that took him over his own home ground. This was in the nature of a farewell to everything dear to him which naturally saddened him even more.

Sun was nowhere to be seen but beautiful blue Earth lay starlit in sleep beneath him and Moon was strongly tempted to shine on her, half hoping she would wake and persuade him to stay where he belonged with his friends, but he lacked courage to speak of his distress to anyone, even to her.

So he travelled on in his troubled state, taking little interest in sights around him and uncaring what course he took.

He dimly saw, but hardly noted, groups of familiar stars in their great constellations but he felt a pang of regret as he passed each of his planetary relations in the Solar System.

Some, like Sun, were asleep; but the warrior Mars - who was at times a trifle aggressive - and mystical Saturn, surrounded by her family circles, both saw Moon and called after him.

Mars, not noticing his sad appearance demanded in his rough but kindly way to know why Moon was upsetting the Solar System by wandering about off his proper course.

But gentle Saturn, more sensitive than her warlike friend, thought that Moon looked sad and lost. Worried, she called after him to ask if all was well.

To these questions Moon could make no reply; he neither felt like speaking with anyone nor knew how to answer their kindly concern for him.

Onward and ever faster, Moon left his familiar world behind. Now almost out of control, pulled this way and that, spinning wildly, he passed planets, other moons and eventually new and unknown stars, some with whole planetary systems of their own.

On rare occasions he was looking forward where he was going but more often he was facing sideways or backward where he had come from. His speed became quite frightening; he never went in a straight line but in swoops and great wheeling curves and often with sudden and violent changes of direction. Had he enjoyed a fuller breakfast he might have been ill with all this bumping and jarring.

Dizzy and frightened, he became quite unable to control where he was heading or to give any attention to his surroundings so, of course, he was soon completely lost.

At times he was speeding through empty space, then suddenly passing horribly close to something that yanked him inward, and just as suddenly flung him with even greater speed off in another direction altogether. Often it seemed he was sure to collide with some great mass ahead of him but, luckily, he sped wildly passed it.

Once he passed right through a seemingly solid body only to find it was a great cloud of gas and cosmic rubbish, leaving him breathless and covered with a horrid dust that he struggled to brush off his face and out of his eyes (which he then decided to keep firmly shut).

He became more and more dishevelled, bruised through

bumping into balls of ice and rock, scorched by flaming stars and sometimes squashed and squeezed as if he was a wheezy concertina like Jupiter's moon Io. Soon he had been so tossed around that he hardly remembered who, or even what, he was.

As the nightmare journey continued, Moon could only cling to his familiar case and concentrate his mind into comforting thoughts of his home and friends, shutting out the horrible reality of the violence about him and the constant fear of what might happen next. But his efforts to keep his mind from failing him were repeatedly upset by violent events.

He thought of Sun, then woosh! – a rock spun past so close that he involuntarily opened his eyes, then immediately closed them to shut out the awful scenes around him. He thought of Earth and bang! - a lump of ice hit him. He turned his mind to his old home and smelt hot gases followed at once by the sudden touch of searing flames.

Each shock was followed by another, then another.

And so the horrific flight continued. For how long, Moon could never tell; it might have been days or weeks. Nightmares last too long however short they may be.

Nothing in the Universe stays unchanged for ever (except, perhaps, the pleasure one gets from a good roast dinner with a nice chocolate pudding to finish) and Moon's hectic and painful journey was no exception.

Eventually his frightening speed slowed right down. In fact he came as nearly to a standstill as a moon can get and found himself in a vast and empty space.

No longer buffeted and bashed by everything that whizzes about in the Universe, from ice to scrap spacecraft and astronauts' lost socks or choked by rude clouds of dust, he risked opening his eyes and took a slow, fearful look around him.

For the first time in a long while he was not being thrown this way and that like a sort of celestial yo-yo. Now, travelling slowly, smoothly, evenly, he could take an interest in his surroundings.

Moon was completely lost with no idea in what direction his old home lay but, strangely, it was also exciting to be in a new adventure and he thought with something like pleasure how awed Sun and Earth would be when they heard of it. This was quickly followed by the sharp and saddening realisation that, as matters stood, none of his old friends would ever know that he had done anything much at all except make a mysterious disappearance.

But, despite this upsetting thought, Moon determined not to sink back into his earlier despair. In fact, being at heart a naturally positive sort, he soon became almost (but not quite) cheerful.

Indeed, he was recovering so much of his self-respect that he cleaned his face and brushed as much of the clinging dust off his nice creamy coat as he could, leaving it a good deal better but still sadly stained and really only fit to wear when he was cooking something unpredictable, like spaghetti. Then, realising that he was very, very hungry (a positive sign in itself), he turned to his awkwardly shaped square case to see what it offered by way of a satisfying meal.

The fact is that Moon was at last on his way to overcoming his imp ridden state, although his imp hadn't finished making trouble for Moon.

After all, that is what imps do, or at least the younger ones. Although why they do it, I really cannot say any more than I can explain why some unpleasant people like to cause trouble wherever they go and always seem to get away with their unkindness. – Have you noticed that?

Now you may remember Moon had stuffed his case with food from his larder so he wasn't short of something to eat but he had also suffered a shockingly violent journey across what seemed like much of the Universe (which is quite a trip for anyone, even Mr Aldrin).

Just as he had suffered a bumpy ride himself, his case had been tossed and tumbled about like some cosmic plaything quite as much as its owner.

And the result was that, when it was opened, all the neat

containers of cakes, biscuits, eggs and bacon, beans, buttery mashed potato and so on had got themselves undone. It was as if Moon's troublemaking imp had been in his case doing horrible spiteful things as such imps will do when they get the chance and think no-one is looking.

In truth the state of the content of Moon's case had everything to do with the violence of its journey. Very little, if any, was down to the unwelcome passenger which was about to make its appearance. The imp had indeed made free of any food it fancied but this was hunger, not nuisance-making at work.

Everything was thoroughly mixed together in one awful and frankly, revolting, mess which did not look in the least appetising, even to someone as hungry as Moon.

One might be prepared to put up with bread that's been spread over with mashed potato but it's an altogether different matter when the plum jam is in there too. And nicely sliced ham is fine with a little cheddar cheese but the addition of a raw egg is enough to make one wish for a dry biscuit and no butter.

For that matter, like most (but not all) of us, Moon greatly preferred his eggs cooked. Something which he now suddenly realised was quite beyond him to do as his stove and cooking utensils had elected not to come with him on his journey, preferring rather to stay behind and mind the home, having a restful holiday while their owner went tumbling around the Universe and only cold food for comfort.

Moon became hungrier, as we all do when we think we are about to get a meal and then have our hopes dashed.

It was also about that time in his regular lunar month phases when he seemed to lose part of his shiny roundness every night. Then, to anyone that looked for him, he appeared more and more like the dwindling segment of an orange than the entire fruit itself, eventually fading to just a circular dark shadow which was hardly visible at all.

Normally when this happened, he treated himself to several extra meals each day until he could see that he had grown back to proper shiny roundness again. Now, in this remote place, as he looked at himself, he saw only a faint shadow and immediately feared for his wellbeing. – This was really no time to be short of food.

Of course we know that Moon doesn't shrink or fade at all as he goes through his phases and that these are all down to the way Sun shines on him. Now, with Sun lost far away, he was bound to seem more shadowy than ever.

But once you suspect you are out of sorts, the thought of a good dinner is likely to perk you up no end. Our friend, being that way inclined (that is, fond of good dinners) treated all his problems, real and imagined, accordingly; that is to say a consequence of being a trifle starved, or to put it another way, starved of a nice trifle.

To cut a long story short (that is shorter than it might have become if it was allowed to wander about to suit itself as if no one had anything else to do but listen to it), Moon did his best to put aside his feeling of disgust at the sight of all his lovely food mixed into a sort of all-purpose stew and set about making up for a number of lost meals.

When he had done this, there was really very little of anything left. He was feeling a little ill and his square suitcase was missing not just a good deal of food but also his comb and toothbrush and some other bathroom necessities.

Moon puzzled over these disappearances but could think of no explanation for them - which he might have done if he had made a connection between them and his sudden indigestion.

A rummage through the debris left in the bottom of his case did, however, bring an unexpected surprise which, whilst unwelcome, helped Moon to complete his recovery. It did not however do anything to improve his temper.

This was the discovery at last of the troublesome imp that had so upset Moon's happy and otherwise largely uneventful world.

Perhaps the little nuisance had lost all its places to hide with the disappearance of most of the case's contents or maybe it just got careless.

Whatever the reason, Moon, whose eyesight is very good,

especially of course in the dark, spotted the imp's black bottom as it struggled to bury itself more deeply in a crumpled macaroon that Moon hadn't quite fancied as part of his meal. Fast as light itself (well, quite quickly anyway), the imp found itself caught and face to face with its victim.

Although evidence of their mischief is found almost everywhere, from spilled sugar on kitchen floors to leaking hot water bottles on cold nights or disappearing socks in spaceships, not many have seen an imp, let alone caught and held one.

Moon had done neither of these things before but, thanks to Earth's and Sun's wise teaching, he was far from ignorant on the subject of imps and what they may do. As soon as he gripped this one, he knew what it was and promptly realised that here was the cause of a lot (if not all) of his recent troubles.

Holding this wretched pest, Moon thought of all the harm it had done.

He recalled what had been happening to him since the fight with his pyjamas and his missed breakfast that same day, his inexplicable ill temper, his feelings of loss as he parted from Sun and his old home, the terrible journey to this empty place. Perhaps worst of all, the spoiling of his precious food.

And what was still to come?

Good tempered as he is, Moon was naturally very annoyed (we could quite properly use a stronger word – like a*g*y - but Moon is a gentle being and, as he will be reading this, we shan't upset him any more than is absolutely necessary for accurately recording his adventures).

But surprisingly, he also felt some relief, for, quite suddenly, he stopped thinking Sun had deserted him, that he wasn't wanted in the Solar System and that he faced a life of loneliness in empty space. Now he knew this was all the imp's doing.

He had been imp ridden. This was like waking from a horrid dream to find that Sun had just called in to his home to share a good breakfast.

Imps are very strong whatever their size (which they can vary at will but is never more than the size of the trouble they are making at any one time). And they are slightly slippery, which makes them very difficult to hold onto.

They are also very clever indeed at escaping.

This they do by a quick wriggle first to one side, then another, and suddenly your captured imp that you thought was safely imprisoned with nowhere to go, has disappeared. All you are left with is a sound like giggling from a long way off.

But Moon was quite ready for any wriggling (or giggling) tricks that might be played on him. Besides he had suffered a very troubled and unhappy time, so he held the imp very tightly by its ears (which were the only handles available for that purpose) and considered what would be the wisest course to take.

First, he thought to put the captive back in his large square case and lock the imp securely where it could no more harm. But it occurred to him this was hardly a permanent solution; it would just mean that the imp stayed with him until, well, until what? Or when?

To these questions Moon could find no answer. Besides he would probably need to use his case again in future and for that it would have to be imp free.

Then he wondered about putting the imp on some distant planet, or, perhaps a speeding comet and leaving it there for good.

But, as we have seen, Moon is a gentle soul and he didn't wish to be so harsh, whatever the justification. He also worried that somehow this pestiferous creature would find a way to return to trouble him again and perhaps be even more spiteful about it. After all, it had found him and got into his home before without even having a key to his front door and might do so again as imps have a good deal of magic about them and need to be treated warily.

Then he had a great idea and, with it, the beginning of a plan came to him. Like all great ideas it was simple.

Why not take the imp back to Sun and Earth and his other

good friends to judge and decide what ought to be done with (or to) it?

Yes, I do agree. He was avoiding a decision, which seems a little feeble on Moon's part, but he really didn't feel that he was up to such a difficult task on his own.

He was probably right. Sun and the others were not just older, but wiser and used to solving awkward problems like imp disposal and how to keep ice cream cold on hot Sundays and even how to keep boiling cream hot on cold Mondays. They would know what to do if anyone did.

At this point and not in any way wishing to pour cold water on Moon's plan, we have to record that he was making much the same mistake as Sun made at about the same time, but a long way off. Involving a lot of your friends in important decision making, like disposing of imps or what to have for supper, will achieve little apart from a headache and a need to lie down in a dark room until your brain has cooled off and your friends have gone home full of your best chocolate cake.

But, right or wrong, the decision was made. He would make the long trip back to friends and home, taking the imp with him.

Now this was not just a big decision but a brave one on Moon's part and it raised several tricky questions. First, how could he keep the imp secure on the journey? Then, in what direction would he travel? – As to this he had no idea whatever nor how long his journey might take.

His third problem was just as difficult as the others; how would he feed himself and (because he was essentially kindly and humane) how could he feed the imp? Indeed, what food did imps eat and how much of it?

Imps of any size can be very troublesome. The bad ones are also bullies (which is much the same thing as being cowards) and, while this one might not be the very worst kind of imp, it was plainly crafty and Moon wasn't going to trust it until he had solid reason to do so.

He also decided to watch out for any strange happenings in the future whether these involved pyjamas or not.

You might well point out that Moon was late in coming to this decision. True, but better late than later. Had he been more alert on the night when his clothes turned against him, he might even now have been sharing dinner in his kitchen with Sun, his only care being whether or not to have a third helping of the beautiful jam pudding that Sun always brought with her on those cheerful occasions.

As to whether the imp could ever become a trustworthy companion, Moon had yet to discover and, just then, he had no idea how he might find out. Perhaps he never would.

If the imp remained troublesome, then in Moon's locked square case it would have to stay.

Chapter 4

Earth sleeps on and on and on...

**This spinning blue sphere; such beauty.
How could it not have a heart?**

Most beautiful of planets, gentle Earth loved all others in the Solar System and was in turn loved by them, from the smallest of moons to the great planets and, of course, by Sun, mother to all. But Moon was Earth's only son and she held him especially dear and precious.

Perhaps it was chance, or Sun's careful protection, that kept Earth in sleeping ignorance of Moon's Great Disappearance and the chaos that followed it - and there was plenty of turmoil on Earth's own surface to cause her distress had she known of it.

The need to protect Earth was understood throughout the Solar System. By unspoken agreement, no one disturbed her. Everyone hoped Moon would return before she awakened.

The people that lived on Earth, however, were very much aware that some disaster was developing and all the more frightening just because the cause was a mystery.

Few of us take the trouble to check the sky each night and make sure Moon is in his proper position. After all, we are very used to him orbiting about, sometimes in one place, sometimes in another and then nowhere at all for a time. To most people no Moon means he is in his lightless phase or simply shining elsewhere for a while.

Of course astronomers and night time burglars with their moon calendars probably check on Moon every day and would know at once if he strayed off his proper course but these knowledgeable people are a minority. So it was that poor Moon's disappearance went largely unremarked on Earth's surface for some time following his imp ridden departure.

It might have been overlooked even longer but for strange and troubling events which, as they happened in daytime, could not have passed unnoticed even by the most unobservant of people.

After the Great Disappearance, Sun's thoughts focussed ever more on Moon, worrying over his fate and whether she would ever see her dear friend again. Her thoughts elsewhere, Sun gave less and less attention to the task of warming and lighting her planets.

On Earth, days became ever darker until, even at noon, it seemed as if violent storms were about to break from the dark steely grey-blue skies. Earth's atmosphere grew colder, thick fogs spread across her still warm seas and drizzling rains fell on land as if they were Sun's own tears.

Worry and growing fear filled people's minds as gloomy days followed moonless nights. A lost moon and a weakening sun were fearful events and beyond understanding.

It is a human tendency to turn to some higher and mysterious power for aid and comfort when faced with catastrophe. The sun has been worshipped by many people since we appeared on the face of our planet. In this dreadful time many turned to her again for help with prayers and, frankly foolish, offerings.

If Sun's attention had not been fully taken up with her worries, she would have been greatly amused by this sudden devotion. But she might have felt more upset than pleased to see people burning perfectly good cakes or throwing their week's wages down wells by way of sacrifices in her name.

Lives on Earth altered but went on. People faced the increasing cold with more and yet more overlayers of clothing until they looked as round as Moon himself and shops had no extra-large sizes left in stock. Sales of skates, skis, sledges, sleds and almost everything that starts with the letter S, except sun cream, boomed.

Skiing holidays in Austria (where it was too cold) were transferred to southern Spain and sunny holidays on the Mediterranean were simply abandoned. Seas froze over and cross Channel swims would have been replaced by Dover to Calais guided walks if anyone had wanted to take part in such frivolous ventures.

Nights without Moon were so dark that burglars were obliged to abandon their usual nocturnal practices and instead to slink about in the daytime mists and rain. After blindly breaking into various unrewarding establishments including court rooms (to the great annoyance of sleeping High Court judges), police stations and prisons, most of them gave up their calling and turned instead to honest daytime work like bank robbery.

One phenomenon was generally held to be the most sinister of all. Save for almost imperceptible rises and falls, tides ceased.

Beaches missed their twice daily clean up in readiness for the next distribution of tourist litter. Smugglers gave up business as their boats stuck firmly on waterless beaches. Small boys stopped fishing from piers that now stood permanently on dry land and several naval captains got themselves court martialled on account of embarrassing navigational errors.

Brilliant astronomers on Earth constantly studied the skies through their powerful telescopes without being able to find Moon, wherever he might have been. All were desperate to come up with a reason for the Great Disappearance and, of course, to prove they had accurately predicted the event before it happened.

After much discussion between these astro-scientists (perhaps wrangling would be a more appropriate word), it was eventually decided that Moon was not a moon at all. He was too small to be a moon, just as Pluto hadn't really been a planet.

Furthermore, Moon had been quite transparent recently – he was evidently fading away and of course real moons cannot fade. If Moon wasn't a moon, then he couldn't be spinning himself about in orbit around Earth. And, to prove it, there he wasn't.

It was agreed by senior astronomers around the globe that they had foreseen this situation some time ago. The General Public had not been told of it in case people became distressed by the thought of Earth having no moon at all when some other planets had more than their fair share.

For their part, politicians claimed they had always known about this. They hadn't spoken in public of Moon's impending elimination through concern this might lead to mass migration away from Earth to planets where there were solid and dependable moons in plenty and tides to be proud of.

But by this time few people were listening either to discredited astronomers or politicians.

Well-satisfied with the apparent success of their efforts to blind everyone with science, one pair of astronomers went on a series of poorly attended but well-paid lecture tours to the warmer regions of the planet speaking on the subject "How the Moon Myth was Finally Exploded". Afterwards both took early retirement and pretended to be out whenever news reporters called for interviews.

What of Earth herself in these harsh times?

She slept on under Sun's protective guard but troubled by dreams in which the night sky seemed over-dark and empty while Earth herself searched for something she could not find in empty cupboards and circular rooms.

At times she dreamt that she was accompanied in her search by some small and friendly creature which struggled to communicate with her; but what it wished to say remained a mystery.

Chapter 5

Advice from far away

Love at first sight? Nonsense, I disliked all my friends on first meeting. In fact I dislike them still.

Lost in a part of space which was peculiarly empty, Moon could see only a few distant stars. As a celestial being himself, he had always been interested in the star constellations of his own night sky and knew a good deal about them but, here, he recognised nothing.

Our own well ordered, predictable night sky is such a familiar (and therefore comforting) part of our surroundings that anything unexpected about it would be very disturbing indeed. Imagine how we would feel if our own skyscape changed entirely between one night and the next. That is just how Moon felt.

For a few moments he was overcome by a new wave of panic such as might engulf anyone whose own world had spirited itself away without a word of apology to make way for another.

To ease his mind he turned his thoughts again to his friends, and especially Sun with her warmth and practical kindness. That calmed him a little. He recalled the fun they had all enjoyed together in their comfortable old world. That cheered him. Then, as if someone had suddenly jogged his memory, he remembered something else, something tangible that he could hold and look at: his wonderful picture of Sun.

Taking this from his case (carefully avoiding any encounter with the captive imp which was evidently asleep or hiding somewhere among the crumbs, cores and crusts), he took a long look at her smiling face.

His panic subsided away altogether as Sun seemed at that moment to speak straight into his mind over whatever vast distance lay between them:

"Dear Moon, my thoughts are ever with you. Never despair; trust your judgement; stick to the decisions that you make and all will yet come right."

Sun's silent telepathic words that day would stay with Moon, not just through his present difficulties but ever afterwards. They gave him a new confidence in himself and he never again felt such deep despair whatever hardships he faced later through his quite adventurous life.

Naturally Sun's advice didn't mean Moon could just sit around and do nothing, waiting for some miracle to come his way.

Nowadays, with so little magic left in this world and so many more people needing a bit of it, miracles have become very rare indeed. If you do wait for one, either it won't come at all or at the last moment it may turn aside and benefit your next-door neighbour just as you thought it was walking up your own garden path armed with all the magic you asked for.

Then where are you? In for another long wait probably.

Luckily Moon (who was very wise himself in his own way) fully understood what his friend meant about trusting his judgement which was simply this:

When you face a knotty problem, make a decision on what to do. Then stick firmly to your plan and follow it to the end.

People who do not, or will not, make decisions achieve nothing apart from waking up the next morning to find yesterday's puzzles still waiting for them. And those that make decisions but keep changing their minds might as well not make them in the first place.

So, noting with some regret that Sun had neglected to point him in the way of a square meal or even just a few toasted sandwiches with a large bowl of mushroom soup and a cake or two, Moon turned with determination to the practical problem of how to make his way home.

Like struggling with the language in a foreign country, most problems are easier, and may even be fun, to solve with a companion on hand. As he slowly sailed along, spinning and thinking, Moon wished he could discuss his difficulties with someone.

He remembered the wretched imp locked in his case but immediately rejected the idea that such a troublesome being would be any sort of use. But, once the thought had occurred to him, it kept returning, reinforced by loneliness and his need for a friend of any sort. After all the imp had no more reason to stay lost in space than Moon.

Unable to stop thinking about this, deciding whether or not to approach his unwanted travel companion became even more important in Moon's mind than the question of how to get home. Eventually of course he just had to try his luck. He made the decision and set his doubts to one side.

Taking hold of the battered old case, Moon tapped gently on the lid to make contact with its inmate:

"Imp, I want to talk to you. If I let you out, will you behave yourself?"

There was no answer.

It had taken real courage for Moon to extend an offer of friendship (or at least a truce) to his persecutor and this lack of response rather put him off trying again. He stayed silent for a while. But, recalling Sun's advice and his recent resolution to stick to decisions once they were made, he wasn't going to give up.

Trying again, he rapped (quite hard this time) on the case and said in a loud voice:

"I want to discuss something with you imp. I need your advice and help. It's for our mutual advantage. Will you help to resolve a problem that affects both of us?"

This, too, enjoyed no reply and, beginning to go a little red in the face and feel rather tetchy, Moon was clearing his throat ready to speak in a very loud voice (let us be honest, it was going to be a shout), when a rather high, almost squeaky, voice said:

"I hope you're not going to shout at me just because you've lost your temper as well as your sense of direction."

The voice sounded very clear and, indeed, close to Moon's ear.

Voices from inside locked cases do not sound clear and, unless the speaker is a ventriloquist, they don't sound close to your head if your case is nowhere near it. Moon was so surprised by this peculiar event that he quite overlooked the rudeness of the speaker and answered in mild tones that he hadn't lost his temper but he was a bit lost in space.

"You are more than a bit lost, I think. And if you want my help, you had best be honest with me!"

This cheekiness was really all too much for Moon who had now recovered from his shock at finding the imp was evidently out and about when it ought properly to have been under lock and key. What was more, the wretched creature was evidently full of bounce and not, as it should have been, reflecting regretfully on its recent misdeeds.

So a fairly hot exchange developed between the two of them.

Had anyone else been close enough to hear it, they might have wondered how such a falling out could be happening when Moon and the imp were hopelessly lost and very likely to stay that way if they persisted in wasting their energies by swapping insults.

Fortunately this row between them came to a sudden end when Moon, who had just been called *"a great cream cheese"* by the imp in response to having in turn been described as *"a silly black beanpole"*, realised how foolish they both looked, saw the funny side and burst into laughter.

It's very difficult to maintain a hot-blooded argument with someone who is rolling about and clutching his sides.

The imp swallowed the next insult it was about to throw in Moon's way, held its breath in an effort not to smile, gave up and collapsed into a laugh that sounded as if some overweight person in a bad temper was trying to inflate a bicycle tyre with a leaky pump whilst grunting and wheezing like the moon Io. (Who wants her name included in this story again as it makes her feel less unloved).

Whether by its deliberate intention or perhaps imps just cannot stay invisible when they laugh, Moon at last got a clear sighting of his companion.

There was the imp, perched on a corner of his battered case and staring back at him as if it felt no shame at all for what Moon had suffered since he had been imp ridden away from his home and friends.

Indeed the imp had no regret whatever, believing, as all young imps do, that the world is made for their amusement, whether the world likes it or not.

Despite the imp's arrogant ways, you won't be surprised that this was the start of much better relations between them. Laughter cures many ills especially ill temper.

Of course Moon was still annoyed by the tricks that had been played on him and the imp was grumpy about its recent captivity even though it had escaped quite easily by means that you will have to work out for yourself. But all things considered, I think we may look upon them as being on the road to becoming friends from this time onward and ever better friends as time progressed.

When he had recovered his breath (laughter always left him short of air and hungry, which is much better than being left short of hair and angry), Moon started wondering again. First, where was the next meal coming from? Next, how might they make the journey home?

On that question we must leave him with his problems because we have to check up on his anxious friends to see if they are likely to come to his rescue and, if so, how, and when?

Chapter 6

Sun at home

When I may not hear your voice or hold your hand, dear friend; enter my dreams.

Authors have a great many tricks up their sleeves which they like to play on their suffering readers. All too many tricks in my opinion; there ought to be a Law for Getting Writers Under Proper Control.

You know the sort of thing I mean: the hero is going along nicely with his adventures. You've just moved on to the next chapter expecting to hear what happened next and how the pirates managed to re-float their ship or if the handsome prince really is a warthog, when, without any warning at all, the writer says something like this:

"So now we must go back in time to learn what the rest of the characters have been doing…"

Just what you don't want to hear – you're torn between throwing your book at the wall or skipping a few chapters to get back to the real action. After all, who wants to go backwards when things get interesting?

In my view authors that do this ought to be sent to corrective writers' school and not allowed out until they promise never to do it again. Keep the main story going and leave the unimportant bits out. That's our motto.

So now we must leave Moon and the imp where they are and go back in time to our familiar, comfortable solar system and learn what Sun and her friends have been doing about Moon's disappearance.

{Well, I didn't promise not to do it and it was just too tempting.}

I'm sorry to tell you that what the friends were doing didn't amount to very much at all.

This was not for any want of care or worry about Moon. Indeed, they were all extremely concerned for their friend. It was due rather to a complete inability to reach agreement on any subject whatever, including even the times and attendant menus for the numerous meals necessary to keep everyone in good round form for their discussions.

Had they each been capable of staying silent long enough to hear what any of the others wanted to say, their meeting might have been more productive.

Indeed it could hardly have been less so. But as we all know, it needs only two loudmouths in a room for any meeting to be a lost cause. Add to these two a further couple who are either asleep or nearly so and what hope have you?

Resisting a temptation to bang a few planetary heads together, Sun at last abandoned her many-heads-better-than-one approach (I did foretell this if you recall) and went on with her day job where she could think without a lot of interruptions and silly suggestions by people with nothing helpful to say, but determined to say it.

When I mention that the suggestions (as to the cause of Moon's mysterious vanishment) had ranged from kidnapping to dematerialisation, you will readily understand Sun's irritation - and Sun is the easiest going of anyone in the Solar System and quite used to the eccentricities of her very varied family.

As she reached the end of her day, Sun had also reached some conclusions (and not just about what to have for dinner, although this was of course one of them).

In her search for Moon she decided, first, that her friends were best forgotten as far as any help was concerned and, secondly, that she must keep as close as possible to Moon in spirit.

Once dinner was over and before suppertime, Sun went back to Moon's circular home hoping for some clue or just for any inspiration the place might provide.

It is after all a well-known fact that clever detectives get nearly all their hunches from a lonely night time visit to the scene of the crime with the murderer watching through a hole in a thick curtain, at the same time fingering something horribly sharp. Well you need something sharp to make holes for looking through thick curtains.

Very little had changed since her sad visit when Sun found the house empty of her friend. She saw however that someone had neatly swept the floors clear of pyjama buttons and tidied up Moon's circular kitchen so that he would feel welcome if and when he returned.

Sun noted this kindly work but rather wished everything had been left as it was.

Detectives always get upset when well-meaning amateurs destroy the evidence, whether by clumsily treading over footprints in the soft soil by the window sill or straightening the corpse's bedclothes. Sun rather wondered if there had ever been any soft soil or rumpled sheets that might have helped to explain Moon's fate.

Something she had missed on her earlier search was the smart little case on the wardrobe floor. Pulling this out and opening it with no expectation it would help her investigation, Sun was surprised to find a frying pan and cooking stove along with quite a variety of other oddments which apparently had nothing much in common.

She thought again of the changes she had seen in the picture on Moon's wall. Sun feared what it might now have to tell, yet she had to know.

Returning to the portrait she forced herself to look. It was hardly recognisable; Moon was just visible as a creamy speck at the edge of sight; Pluto had gone; her own portrait had shrunk and dimmed as if it had lost all its inner glow; only Mars remained as his old substantial self. She could detect no movement in the picture.

If there was any comfort to be drawn from this, it was that Moon had not yet disappeared altogether. Sun resolved that she would not look at the picture again – it was just too distressing.

Again, she sat herself down in the circular rocking chair and rolled slowly around Moon's familiar room. As she rolled, she drifted into thought and as she thought she drifted into sleep and thence into dreams which flowed seamlessly from their parent thought.

First Sun thought of the small case, then of its contents and then of what was missing from Moon's belongings in his home. She tried to imagine what events could explain all the evidence and, so doing, she slept.

The dream began quite gradually as if Sun were floating like a gentle spirit through the rooms of Moon's home, observing, sensing the atmosphere, reaching out to him. In that dream someone who did not look at all like Moon, but Sun knew to be him, came into the room and sat down for a while in thought so deep it seemed that time stood still. Then, rising, the Moon spirit took out two travel cases and packed them both with no apparent thought or care.

If Sun had been uncertain she was dreaming of Moon, the fact that this spirit was filling its cases with food and cooking equipment left no room for any doubt. Only Moon would pack so much to eat and leave nearly all his clothes behind for a considerable journey, and he clearly expected to travel far.

Its packing done, the dream spirit wandered around Moon's home going into each circular room for a time and standing in apparent reflection before suddenly vanishing.

Sun slept on, now dreamless, until she woke just in time to paint a new dawn in bright pinks and golds by way of contrast to her disturbing dream and a sign of optimism for the benefit of everyone after another moonless night.

On the day following her dream Sun could not stop thinking of Moon and the spirit seen in her sleep. She felt drawn back to his home, wanting to sit again in the same chair; to re-enter the dream; if possible, to make some communication with her friend.

As the day progressed, these thoughts took stronger hold. Sun's concentration on her day's regular tasks waned; she shone dimly; her brilliance faded and, taking advantage of Sun's neglect, cold mists spread across Earth's skies. By sunset, her realm was unusually dark.

As another night came without Moon's gentle light, everywhere on Earth lay in deepest shadow; for remote stars' tiny lights of guidance have no power to illuminate anything more than themselves.

By her standards, Sun's meals that day had been very modest, not to say frugal, but for once she had no thought for food.

After dark fell, having made only a sketchy twilight sky in tones of cloudy grey (to the great disappointment of three artists who had paid a substantial sum each for their sunset-illustration-and-moonlight-on-the-water painting courses), she hurried to Moon's silent home, settled in the familiar chair and waited for whatever would come.

She had no fear of the unknown, just eager anticipation.

Fate was less than kind. Sun could not sleep and the Moon spirit was elsewhere, if indeed it existed at all.

But, late in the night, near to the time when Sun would have to make the new dawn sky, she fell into a doze - the sort when you are unsure if you are awake or dreaming and probably you are doing both.

It seemed that someone was reaching out to her, trying to tell, or ask, something but what that was she barely understood.

In her half sleeping state she heard herself speaking, saying some words like *"We must all stick to our decisions, Moon my dear"*. But, although she woke almost at once, she could not remember her exact words and the harder she tried, the less clearly she recalled them until it seemed she might have imagined the whole episode.

That little was all Sun could achieve in making contact with her lost friend despite several more attempts in subsequent nights.

But she felt more comforted than she might have hoped. At least Moon had evidently left by his own choice – you don't stop to pack a case if you are being kidnapped or dematerialised so those two ridiculous suggestions at least could be discounted.

But this was as far as Sun's thoughts could take her. Moon's home seemed to offer no more by way of clues and there are just so many nights you can spend waiting for ghostly visitations that do not happen.

After all, spirits probably have a lot of other important things to do apart from teasing their old friends - like scaring people who are foolish enough to visit old castles at midnight and drunken farmers who need to be turned into jabbering idiots for a day or two, if not longer. A ghost's life is mostly hard work, for such tasks need dedication and time, if not a university degree in some suitable subject like mortuary management.

Having turned over in her mind all that she knew of Moon's departure, Sun felt her head buzzing and circling like the sort of bee that comes uninvited to a picnic on a summer's day and just won't take the hint it isn't wanted.

She decided to talk again with her solar family, or at least the more sensible ones.

After the last experience when she had gathered them altogether – and regretted it, she approached them individually and did her best to stop any of the Nuisance Brigade from barging into the conversation. This was not easy as those with the least useful to say were, of course, keenest to say it and as loudly as possible so as to emphasise their point as silly people always do. – You noticed that too?

Sun would have started by speaking with Earth but Earth had, as usual, been asleep on the day of Moon's disappearance and remained unaware of it. There was nothing to be got from waking her except an inevitable description of Moon's admirable qualities since birth *"which had always been obvious to everyone when he was growing up and showing such promise ..."* and so on and on.

No, it certainly wasn't worthwhile waking Earth just for that.

Avoiding having to listen to a flow of such motherly nonsense, Sun proceeded to speak with most of the rest of her larger planets in turn. (She omitted Jupiter who takes so long to reply to any question, one might as well talk to a ball of gas and the wheezy answer, when and if it does arrive, is usually not worth getting from him, poor chap).

This circuit of Sun's relations produced two startling and similar pieces of information from Saturn and Mars respectively. Both claimed they had seen the departing Moon and his baggage; both had asked why he was so far off his proper orbit and neither of them had got a reply.

As to Moon's direction, Saturn said one thing, Mars another. Just the lack of observation one might expect of one planet that spends half its time doting on its family circles and the rest asleep and another planet that is nearly always getting angry with something or other when awake.

Sun, getting even hotter under her collar (well, she doesn't of course have a collar actually and if she had, it would have burst into flames long ago), wanted to know how the blazes this information had been kept back until now.

Mars, being what he is, said in a very loud voice, - sufficiently loud for the entire Solar System (and then some) to hear - that he had tried to tell everyone at the earlier planetary meeting but no-one was listening.

Having her own memories of that unsatisfactory assembly, Sun could quite believe this so she muttered something about wishing *"some people would stay a little calmer"* and left Mars to enjoy his little victory.

But from Saturn, Sun did learn something else that first worried, then puzzled, her and eventually led to reaching a surprisingly accurate explanation of what had befallen poor

Moon. For Saturn, despite her other-worldliness had seen that Moon was lost, abstracted and plainly very sad as he passed by on his obscure journey that day.

Moon had left alone and apparently unhappily so, Sun reasoned, he left unwillingly. The question remained "What made him go?"

Feeling again a need for help, Sun returned that evening to Moon's deserted home and sat once more in his favourite circular chair.

Rocking herself gently back, forth, then over and over, she fell into a dreamlike state in which she was carried away to the day when Moon left that very room to sail over sleeping Earth and later to be seen by irate Mars and kindly Saturn, a sad and distracted figure going … well, who knows where, or why?

Half dreaming, half awake, Sun thought of Moon's good cheer, his laughter, his love of practical jokes and games of any kind. How could such a being be brought so low and so suddenly?

The problem ran round and round in Sun's mind and she slipped into deep and then deeper sleep.

At first she dreamt nothing, then came a happy scene in which she sat down with Mars and Saturn to a huge dinner with Moon, who had just returned from somewhere far away accompanied by a strange friend. In the usual unhelpful way that dreams have of teasing people, it failed to tell where Moon had been and gave no information at all about his companion.

This dream slipped quickly and completely away and, as dreams often do, it ran into the next which displaced it without bothering to explain the connection between the two, if there was any.

Sun's last dream that night was more unusual and harder to understand. After waking she retained only a memory of a great dish full of mixed foods in which a small creature burrowed and giggled as it munched.

She was inclined to put this troubling scene down to a

shortage of recent meals and immediately began to put right that deficiency. The memory of this curious dream, however, stayed with her, adding itself to the rest of the facts and mysteries she was accumulating about the Great Disappearance, as it was now called within the solar fraternity.

Chapter 7

Martian dream

Helpful friends – ah, what a blessing they might be – but, I ask: Are any to be found?

As we have seen, Sun's meeting broke up with nothing agreed, no plan, nothing much to eat and more than a little irritation on the part of those present.

Sun having gone on her way to make her own plans for rescuing Moon from whatever fate he had suffered, Mars spent some time in thought before speaking to Saturn:

"Sun doesn't seem very pleased about something – I think you must have upset her with your stories Saturn. But I don't hold that against you, she was always a bit tetchy."

To which Saturn replied

"Really Mars, that's a bit twisted even for you. It was you that annoyed her with all that stuff about seeing Moon flitting off who knows where. You had better have kept silent, like me."

But Mars had more on his mind than Sun's feelings:

"Well, you may be right and perhaps we ought to have kept that to ourselves.

I've been thinking that no-one else is going to do anything practical – Sun's not thinking straight and the others are either eating or thinking about food all the time; it's really quite disgraceful when all the while poor old Moon may be drifting and lost anywhere in space and probably not a single chocolate cake within a light year, if not a parsec."

"So what are you trying to say Mars? Is this leading up to another of your crackpot adventures? 'Mars and Co to the Rescue with a fresh cake for Moon' or some such. If so, say what's on your mind and then we can all go back home."

"No need to get upset Saturn, you must try to keep calm always, like me.

I was just going to suggest that we (that is you and I and maybe a moon or two) really ought to have a bit of a glide along the direction Moon was taking when we saw him and see what we can find out. Sun will be awfully pleased with us."

"Mm, I'm not sure Sun will be at all pleased to have us going off course and sending the whole solar system into a wobble, especially if we get lost as well. We only have one Sun and she won't be able to hunt for three missing persons on top of having all her other jobs."

Mars said nothing for some time but he wasn't going to allow his idea to die stillborn.

"Come, Saturn, we must do something, not just for Moon but for our great friend, Sun. We alone saw Moon leaving on his journey. He wasn't happy. Something had gone horribly wrong.

We ought to rescue him and punish whatever or whoever was at the bottom of it."

Saturn felt she didn't want to punish anybody although she did want very much to help Moon.

Yet she cared for her own numerous moons, from the rocky fragments to great Titan and if she accompanied Mars, they must of course all come with her. She could hardly leave them behind orbiting around nothing, but for her to go wandering about with her entire retinue whizzing in rings around her head was unthinkable. Mars really was crackbrained at times.

"No, I'm sorry Mars, I can't come with you and I don't think you should

*leave your orbit and go off on your own. Heaven knows how the rest of us
will be affected if you move out of place.*

*Everyone's tracks will be affected; it was bad enough with Moon leaving
and you're a great deal larger. We all depend on one another to stay
predictable."*

*"Predictable! By my spear and shield, a bit of a wander by us will shake
up the lot of them. Do them good! I'm going anyway."*

*"You forget, Mars, that Sun confiscated both your spear and shield after
the last episode – yes, I know, that asteroid was very cheeky and quite
deserved a good prod but you're altogether too warlike sometimes. And
we don't even know that Moon has been harmed; he just looked a bit
miserable. At least discuss all this with Sun before you act."*

Mars made a noise that sounded like *"Sun's a softy"* but might have
been something a good deal ruder. We had best not inquire too
deeply.

Mars wasn't intending to travel alone in his search; his own moons
would be going with him but this was not a prospect that any of
them relished as much as you might suppose.

Mars' moon, Deimos, is a true chip off the old block. Just as
belligerent as its planet, the two of them had been in a constant
state of mutual annoyance for several million years. Contrast that
with not speaking to your best friend and neighbour for a week.

His other moon, Phobus, is ever silent; we happen to know it
has its own problems – something to do with declining and it's
terminal, so we mustn't be critical.

The original cause of the differences between Mars and his
awkward moon is long forgotten but these two were so used to
arguing that it was a matter of course, even pride, that they both
made use of any new event to fall out once more.

There were occasional periods of peace, if not much goodwill, between them. A good feast would put them in more friendly humour and, of course, a game of Bowls - provided they were on the same team. On those rare occasions when they played for opposing sides, they were sure to set light to each other within the first five minutes of the match.

The conversation with Saturn had of course been heard by Mars' moons. Phobus as ever said nothing, but its companion had seen the opportunity for another row:

"Do not suppose that I shall come with you willingly on this ridiculous adventure, Mars, you old idiot. If you force me to, I'll give you no help whatever. I shall come merely for Moon's sake and to watch you make an even bigger fool of yourself than usual."

"Your obstruction will be nothing unusual, you shapeless lump. You will come with me; not because I need you but I can't leave you mooning about in space, tripping up anything that comes by and frightening honest planets with your horrible appearance."

So they bickered on as Mars set about preparing for his venture to help Moon. In his packing he was almost as incompetent as Moon had been partly because the most important items for the journey were his spear and shield which Sun had taken away from him.

Mars felt he must have these "to deal with" whoever or whatever had so upset his friend.

Taking a little time to consider this problem, Mars decided he simply had to recover his weapons and, as he was sure Sun would disapprove of his intended venture, this would have to be achieved by stealth.

Mars isn't very good at sneaky things like stealth but the alternative of guile was a non-starter as he has little or no skill in persuading others with mere words.

Mars set off for Sun's vast home while Sun herself was high in the mid-day sky doing a little quiet thinking of her own about Moon's disappearance and wondering if she might reach him through her thoughts.

Entering Sun's house (which was never kept locked as its owner didn't believe either in privacy or burglars), Mars at once realised the task of finding his property was almost certainly beyond him unless he struck lucky. The place was just too large to search; his spear might be anywhere.

I should mention at this point that, had Mars been more observant, he would have seen that both his spear and shield were standing in the place where he usually kept them. Sun had quietly returned both on the day after the episode with the asteroid when she had taken them away briefly for everyone's safety.

Being at a loss where to look for his property and tired from the frustrations of a stressful day, Mars sank into one of Sun's vast rocking chairs and gazed vaguely at some of her paintings.

Her artistic skill was really amazing, going far beyond skies and her numerous mouth-watering culinary subjects.

Mars was very attracted by a series of cream cake studies and realised he was quite hungry.

Suddenly he forgot about food as his attention was taken by a group picture of Sun herself (she had no false modesty), her planets (of course Pluto was there – how could you ask?) and a selection of moons – only some of these because there are far too many in the Solar System to include them all in one illustration.

Mars was struck by the obvious happiness of everyone in the group.

Looking more closely he saw the title – "Happy Day with Friends" and as he read this it seemed the picture came alive; the subjects slowly rotated and orbited in his imagination. He heard them talking among themselves, unaware they were watched. Indeed Mars himself was in the group, moving with them, conversing with his good friend Saturn.

It was all too strange; he tried to clear his mind; realised he was half, if not fully, asleep; abandoned the fight to stay awake and slipped fully into his dream.

The conversations coming out of Sun's picture mostly concerned a recent Bowls match; apparently one where Jupiter had squashed some unfortunate moon before himself being ignited by something that looked a bit like an enormous ant.

Mars studied this strange being but could not recognise it; perhaps it lived in some remote part of the Milky Way; he felt sure it wasn't from Sun's world. Whatever it was, it was a very good Bowls player and Mars liked it for that.

The scene changed slowly. Planets and moons in the picture disappeared one by one. Mars did not see them leave but each time he rotated someone else had gone and the sky was less full.

Eventually only Sun, Moon, Saturn, the strange Bowls player and Mars himself were left together. Voices from those who had left could be heard in the distance. Mars wondered if the party in the picture was still going on somewhere else without them.

Their surroundings changed suddenly in that believable way that dreams have of achieving the impossible without the least apology or explanation.

Each member of the group became very small; they were now standing on a great green surface; above them a light blue sky with a few high, streaky clouds. Instantly, Mars knew this could be only one location; it was Earth's surface, an unattainable place of miracles and beauty, surpassing everything else in the Solar System.

The green surface developed into grass, trees, flowers and Mars delighted in it all, yet it seemed his companions were less affected as if they had been there before.

The Bowls player was speaking; something about needing rules in the Game; Mars did not much like the sound of that and was about to say so but the others moved on and he had to hurry to catch up, strangely and unusually fearful of being alone and lost in this miraculous place.

When he caught up, only Saturn and the Bowls rule maker (as Mars now thought of it) were left.

By unspoken agreement, they stopped among a group of trees. The little orchard was full of life, vigour, sound and colour; complex, wonderful and outside Mars' experience and understanding. The rule maker was saying something but Mars was too absorbed in his surroundings to pay attention.

They stood silent for a while on that bright and windy day, each with their own thoughts, then they walked on together leaving the cherry trees behind but taking with them memories of that place which would never fade.

Often in the future Mars would return there in his dreams. Whenever he did, no warlike thoughts ever entered his mind; he was, at those times and always for some days afterwards, completely at peace with himself.

"Hallo Mars! How nice of you to call! I'm just going to have a spot of lunch. Come and sit at the table."

Meeting her at that moment, no-one who did not already know would have guessed the depths of Sun's distress in that hard time. The smile was almost as broad as ever and the voice as cheery. Well, perhaps very slightly quieter.

The dream vanished, leaving an incomplete memory of its passage; Mars was a little resentful and also guilty that he should feel that way about Sun of all his friends. Then he remembered why he had come there in the first place and felt ashamed; a rare experience for robust, self-confident Mars.

Sun asked no questions but busied herself preparing what she would have described as a modest snack and talking cheerfully about nothing in particular until:

"You won't find your spear here Mars; I took it back to you some time ago. I'm surprised you haven't found it – your shield too."

Mars muttered something inaudible.

"You know, it won't do for you to go looking for Moon. In the first place you don't know where he is and in the second, by the time he's back here you will be lost yourself and I shall have another cause for worry. My problem is that I love you all too much."

"I suppose my wretched moon has been babbling to you. I shall have

something to say in that quarter when I return."

"Nothing of the sort, Mars, I'm quite capable of working things out myself without using spies and for your information, your moon is much too loyal to tell tales about you.

Now promise me you will stay in your proper place. You can be far more help here."

Sun got her promise, reluctantly, and after their meal together, Mars felt he had to speak to someone about his dream and no-one better than wise Sun. So he described all that he could recall of it while Sun listened in silence, staring at her own painting and wondering if she could really have forgotten to include her dear Moon. When he finished, Sun had questions to ask but Mars had little more that he could tell her.

"You say Moon was there in my picture; are you sure? Because he doesn't seem to be there now. And where did this Bowls player come from? Was it with Moon at any stage in your dream?"

Mars was both sure and unsure of his memory.

"I can see he isn't there now but Moon was certainly in your painting when I first looked into it – anyway you wouldn't have missed him out of the group, would you?

I don't know where the rule maker thing came from, but it knew how to play; I'd like to have it on my team. I think it was with Moon from the beginning, in fact I got the impression they were friends – strange but there it is."

"And," continued Mars *"It's probably all nonsense; I don't believe in dreams; just thought you ought to know about this one. We'd all be doing better by searching for Moon, not sitting around talking about twaddle."*

Recalling her own dream, Sun wondered if the being she had seen there was the same as the stranger described by Mars but she said nothing of this. Mars is brave, open and honest but not a planet to choose for confidences.

What she needed was a trustworthy helper she could send out to search for Moon or any sighting of him. This was definitely not Mars; it had to be small, far off (as the Solar System goes) and discrete. There was just one obvious choice.

She spoke of this to no-one except her chosen aide.

Sun sat still and silent for so long that, being a doer, not a thinker, Mars began to fidget and, being circular, he also began to feel hungry again.

It's like that when you're in Sun's home, so much eating goes on there and the food is so good, that, when not actually involved in the middle of a meal, no truly round being can avoid thinking hopefully about what might be next on the menu. Perhaps it has something to do with the faint smell of baking.

Having read his thoughts, Sun smiled gently at her guest. Going out to her kitchen, she returned in ten minutes or so with a great tureen of soup, a good pile of toast-and-something snacks, the inevitable massive chocolate cake, a tray of her own pastries and a vast pot of coffee.

"This dream of yours – it has to be good news, rather than bad.

First of all we have to decide if it comes from the past or the future. Since none of us knows about this Bowls-rule making thing, we can't have met it yet so this is about the future.

Second, you saw Moon with this rule-maker, so they both existed at the same time. Lastly, you were in the group with them which seems to tie everyone together. I believe that means we shall be seeing both of them, hopefully soon."

Sun paused for a moment as worries filled her mind again but Mars noticed no change in her ever-cheerful face.

"I don't think we can take it any further since you seem to have forgotten the rest of your dream which was a bit careless of you, Mars. – I wonder if Saturn has a dream to tell us about."

Being rather nettled by Sun's comments, Mars felt a need to recover his dignity.

"Well, I hope you're right Sun but it's your fault I don't remember any more because you would come barging in and waking me at just the wrong moment."

"Fiddlesticks! You're always trying to blame someone else when things go astray; you should learn to take responsibility for your mistakes Mars. Do have another doughnut."

Realising he had the choice between trying to win an argument against Sun (always impossible) and having another of her most excellent pastries (ever a pleasure), Mars wisely took a large fresh, warm doughnut and two vast chocolate eclairs to go with his third coffee while Sun smiled on him lovingly.

"Try not to worry too much Mars, if true (and I believe it is) then your dream is as hopeful a sign as we could wish for. Thank you for telling me of it."

Mars felt quite proud at this; it was always cheering to please Sun. He forgot that he had come uninvited for the purpose of secretly stealing back his weapons and he also forgot that Sun plainly knew it.

No more was said on the subject and, after a few words of farewell, they parted. Mars went away expecting to be criticised by his awkward moon but untroubled by the thought.

Sun on the other hand for some strange reason did something very rare for her.

She sank into Mars' chair and cried - quite alone. Not for the first time, nor the last.

"So you didn't get your spear but spent the time scoffing the contents of poor Sun's kitchen. I hope she gave you a good ticking off."

Unusually, Mars did not react at all as his moon expected him to.

"No, Deimos, I don't have my weapons, in fact they were returned some time back. Sun was her usual lovely self but a little quieter.

And I'm not going to go chasing after Moon so you need not be worried about accompanying me. We shall stay here together and hopefully be happier for it."

Deimos stayed dumbstruck for a moment, then:

"What's got into you then? Earlier you were all set for another fight over nothing. Now suddenly I don't quite know you."

"It's something Sun said about this and that, dreams and loyalty and so on. – I think we need to try understanding each other better."

For once, his moon had no words to say in reply but the two of them were not quite so harsh with one another through the rest of that day and, to their own surprise, they were both slightly more friendly on the next.

Whether this happy improvement continued into the future is another matter; this is a history about a moon and an imp, not an irritable red planet and its troubled satellites.

Chapter 8

Adventures and friendship

You never heard him say "No more cake for me!"

As I was saying earlier, you have to watch out for authors. They can be tricky, especially when they break off in the middle of something exciting, like pirates doing horrible piratical things or ghosts ganging up on the vicar who has got himself locked in his vestry.

These wretched writers will suddenly force their readers, struggling and kicking, back to some previous time and place.

There they start a new story when the poor reader (or readers if the author is luckier than he deserves to be) is (or are) desperate to know where the pirates are going to bury the treasure or if the vicar will be rescued in time or suffer some delightfully gruesome end.

Well, there shall be no such trickery here and to make sure, we shall in future avoid all mention of both pirates and vicars (in their vestries or elsewhere), unless of course they happen to pop in unannounced.

And of course unannounced popping-in is quite beyond any author's control.

We must now go back in time and to another place to see how Moon and his new acquaintance (we cannot yet quite call the imp a friend – that is still a little way off) are progressing in getting away from wherever they are and going somewhere else, wherever that may be.

Unless you are setting out on a mystery tour by bus, it's a good idea to know where your journey's start and end will be. Otherwise you are likely to get into quite serious difficulties about directions, distances and meals on the way.

When Moon started his travels, he knew where he was but had no idea where to go. Now he knew where to go but not where he was starting from.

The imp was in no better position; it had come along largely by accident and partly for the pleasure of being impish.

Having spent much of the trip being jumbled about in Moon's case and not being able to keep track of where they were going, it was now in just the same difficulty as Moon: lost, with no one new to torment, nothing much to eat and only a lot of empty space to look at.

So, if Moon was travelling back to Sun and the Solar System, the imp very much wanted to go along. After all, next to its family home, it was the only other place it knew. A sort of second home in fact.

Now Moon had been hoping the imp would have some useful plan for managing their return and the imp had been relying on Moon for the same, so, having first agreed where to go, they each stared hopefully at the other, and silently waited … and waited … and …

It was all very well to sit there enjoying silence and a little company but Moon felt things must move on. So, after a few minutes (or it may have been hours) of staring and waiting, he said to the imp:

"Well, we must get on with this.

What direction do we follow for the trip back? How long will it take and where's the best and closest place to get some food?

I don't mind telling you I'm very hungry, I've missed a lot of meals. You can see how thin I am – almost invisible in fact."

As the imp was just about to say almost exactly the same thing (apart from the invisibility problem) it felt rather annoyed that it hadn't got in first and was naturally very alarmed to learn that Moon was as lost as it was. Trying to avoid admitting this ignorance, it replied:

"I am of course very happy to help return you to your friends but you are a great deal larger and, I think, older than I am.

It really wouldn't be proper for me to push my way in, so please carry on, take the lead and just tell me what to do.

Oh, by the way, you don't look thin to me, rather the opposite in fact."

Having had the tables turned on him so effectively, Moon sat silent again for a few more minutes, then:

"I'm afraid you assume too much, imp.

First of all, I'm not that old.

Secondly, this is a part of space I haven't visited very often recently so I must rely on your great skill and travel experience to get us moving in the right direction please.

And, by the way, a good square (or round) meal is now quite urgent so don't forget to stop at the earliest opportunity."

I need say no more about this conversation, save to tell you that it ran on for a long while and - not for either the first or the last time - they became rather upset with each other.

Although they would never have admitted it, they were upset also with themselves as neither of them had any idea whatever about directions, distances, time or takeaway food shops on the way.

The prospects for getting home were looking bleak and worse still for getting there without starving first.

They had just reached the stage in their discussion at which insults start to push good manners out of the window when all management of their journey was whisked out of their hands and further discussion about navigation, let alone which were the best restaurants to try, became pointless.

Whilst they had been silently staring at each other and later "exchanging views" (as polite people call arguing) they (that is Moon, the imp, the battered case and anything else that might have become stuck to either of them) had been drifting.

At first, they had drifted slowly, but then with increasing speed, out to the edge of this empty and peaceful part of space.

Eventually they arrived where it was neither empty nor quiet but any amount of speeding and spinning celestial items were exercising their forces, large and small, in pulling and pushing each other and sometimes rudely colliding whenever any two or more of them refused to get out of the way.

Taken up with the important task of arguing in ever louder voices, neither Moon nor the imp had noticed what was happening.

Then, both of them having run out of breath for the moment, a speeding lump of rock whizzed past so close that, if it hadn't been holding on to the lapels of Moon's nice round (but dusty) suit in order to emphasise some point, the imp would have been whisked away from Moon and lost into another story altogether.

Fortunately for the imp, and the rest of us, this did not happen. It has to be admitted however that Moon had felt a slight relief (but only for a moment and to be regretted at once) when it seemed the imp might be about to set off on some unplanned travel of its own.

Also, he reminded himself, he had determined to stick to his decisions and that included taking this imp with him on his journey to the Solar System.

Having spent a lot of time, and wind, debating (or rowing, if you prefer) over how to set about their journey to Moon's home and where, what and how often to eat, they had failed to see how their surroundings had changed. Worse, they had also lost control of their direction and speed. Now they were going who knows where and powerless to do anything but let fate have its way.

As the forces all around them were far too great and numerous to be resisted, they would have been powerless anyway. But it is always comforting to believe you control your own affairs, even though most of us can't do this most of the time and some of us are just helpless always.

Conscious of this helplessness as he was whisked away, Moon had just enough time to recall his promise to stick with his decisions and immediately regret that this was all very well in theory but little use when decision making is rudely torn out of your hands.

That was the last occasion when he had the opportunity to give thought to anything more than survival for quite some time. This new journey promised to be just as bad as Moon's outward trip had been, if not worse.

On the way out, his mind had been so full of his problems that he had been almost indifferent to the violent turmoil of it all and the uncertainty of what would happen when he got wherever he was going.

Now it's a strange thing that, if we are lost in unhappy thoughts on a dull winter day, we don't expect good things to happen.

On such occasions we hardly notice if we forget to open the front door before going out or absent-mindedly stick a finger in the hot toaster to get the bread out when it's got stuck. But, on a fine bright day with our minds alert to the wonderful world around us, little incidents, like hot porridge down the front of one's trousers just before leaving for work at the office, are liable to upset us a lot more.

So it was for Moon. A short while ago he had been cheerfully looking forward to his friends and home (and any number of good round meals) and, not quite so happily, arguing with his companion. In almost no time he was now speeding out of control, feeling thoroughly scared of what was to come and all the more because it was completely unexpected.

The violence of the outward journey had frequently been frightening but this was one long unrelieved nightmare.

Time and again Moon and the imp both felt that their insides were being left behind as first one, then another, violent power grabbed them and jetted them to yet greater speed. Just as often some opposite force would slow them down so suddenly that their digestive systems went on ahead to wait for them to catch up.

The experience was like being on a super-sized fairground ride with occasional brief moments of quiet.

They came to dread those quiet periods more than anything for the fear of not knowing what would come next. Whether violent acceleration or slowing, they seemed always to guess wrong with the result the experience, when it came, was even more frightening.

Their changes of direction were so frequent and unpredictable that they could only stare wildly at each other, hold on tightly and hope that each twist or turn might be the last they would suffer, only to be thrown about again just a few moments later.

While they were tumbled and spun about, there was hardly a minute in which they had a settled view in any one direction. At one moment they were facing one way, the next they were violently turned to look somewhere else. Unable to steady their sight, they were permanently dizzy, unwell and quite incapable of sensible thought.

For some reason no matter how one goes, by car, train, plane, spaceship or foot, travel is always tiring. If the journey is also a rough one it will be exhausting and so it was for our friends.

Tossed and thrown around, frightened, hungry and lost, they each repeatedly fell into exhausted asleep and almost at once woke as they careered on in a seemingly infinite journey through unfamiliar space. For all they knew, they might have been travelling in the wrong direction, going ever further from home.

This scary turmoil went on for days; or was it weeks? They had no idea of how much time had passed since their journey began.

And all the while they were followed. Shadowed by something that stayed just a little too far off to be seen, even if they had been capable of giving attention to anything beyond survival.

At last their direction stopped changing every few moments, that sensation of having someone else's stomach to care for faded away and their speed steadied. Surprisingly, it was almost peaceful. They were travelling very fast; there were numerous stars to see but still no recognisable constellation.

Despite the calmer travel, Moon felt uncomfortable with that sort of unease that comes from being secretly watched by unfriendly eyes. He fought down this irrational fear, firmly turning his mind to practical things - what course to follow, food and care of the young imp,

With a struggle he managed to free the imp's frightened (and painful) grip on him. Eased a little, he steadied his mind and thought.

Moon thought about the journey they had made so far but this gave him no comfort. He was still lost, with no idea either where his recent flight had taken him or where he had started from. In short, he was in a worse situation than ever for deciding their route home. And he was still largely unable to control either his course or speed.

Next, he thought of food; imagining wonderful meals from the past was not unpleasant but it was very unsatisfying.

His mind moved on to consider his companion who just then seemed to be awake but silently and permanently frozen to Moon's once fine creamy coloured coat.

Moon's first thought on seeing this was to leave well alone as there were clear advantages in having a silent imp on board as opposed to a chatty and cheeky one. But he was immediately ashamed of thinking so unkindly.

The imp was on its own and very young, far younger than Moon and apparently without family or friend. He had decided it was his duty to protect his companion and, following Sun's advice, Moon would always hold firmly to that decision.

In fairness to Moon I ought to mention that adopting the job of imp caring was to try his patience severely on several future occasions (and some of them not far off just now). Yet to come were the practical jokes, the pompous rudeness to strangers, the cheekiness...

Ah well, life is never straightforward and they say we are never set problems that are beyond us to solve, although that thought would not have comforted Moon just then.

So, his decision having been made, by way of apology for his earlier ungracious thought, Moon quietly set about calming and cheering his friend.

If you wish to comfort someone, it doesn't do to start with:

"Buck up, you fool! You look a frightful mess. The world won't care if you sit there feeling sorry for yourself. Stop all that self-pitying nonsense; stand up, tell a few jokes and be sure to make everyone laugh."

Although this was what Moon might have liked to say, being a sensitive sort of being, he felt it was a little short on kindness so, instead of the "snap out of it" approach, he said:

"Well, imp, we can be glad that's over. I'm astonished that you look so neat and tidy after all that jostling about.

I expect the rest of the journey will be a lot less bumpy and we shall be stopping for lunch soon. Do tell me what food you would like to have when we get there."

He couldn't have chosen his words better. Imp's love of food was almost as strong as Moon's and it was so desperately hungry that it jumped at the opportunity to talk about lunch menus as the next best thing to having a plate of real food to eat.

There began a happier, but strange, time in which the pair exchanged descriptions of their favourite lunches, dinners, high teas and suppers.

Despite all its adolescent faults, the imp was a surprisingly good cook and no-one has better kitchen skills than Moon. It wasn't long before they were swapping family recipes, mostly for their favourite food. (You need hardly ask; cakes and pastries, of course).

As they talked of meals, so they turned to discussing points of etiquette and the curious table manners of both guests and hosts.

The imp had a particular dislike for guests who say their meal looks just like something they recently bought ready prepared from a supermarket. It also resented the sort of diners who make themselves important (more accurately described as being a nuisance) by claiming to have some allergy which makes it impossible for a host to contrive a menu to suit both them and the rest of the invited guests.

Of course the simple solution to troublemaking by diners is to throw them out there and then and leave them off all future invitation lists. But, as the imp said, it is far more fun to wait for a return invitation and do the same to them.

The imp did not however make any mention of its practical jokes which all too often occurred at meal times. Moon had yet to learn about these.

On his part, Moon described how, at dinners in his own home, he contrived to keep the peace between Mars and almost everyone else. We must, however, allow that to remain Moon and the imp's secret as Mars will be reading this one day and we don't wish to upset the old boy by suggesting his friends manipulate his temper.

Nor will we let him into secrets it is better that he does not know.

As they talked and at times laughed together, so friendship between them grew. A strange mixture of two beings in a strange place and a relationship founded in an unlikely beginning.

Their recent hectic journey had tired both our travellers. As they talked the imp became quieter, then fell into sleep – a sleep in which it dreamt of having a home and a great round friend …

Moon watched the sleeping imp for a while with a growing feeling of kindness toward his small companion and, not unnaturally, also a growing desire for food. Then he, too, slipped into sleep and, for once, he did not dream at all.

They travelled on, more smoothly now, unconscious of speed or direction and, for that brief time, untroubled by either hunger or their fear of the unknown that beset them when awake.

Waking again, but not much refreshed, the travellers talked some more.

Keeping firmly to the task he had undertaken, Moon asked the imp about its family and friends and to tell how it came to be alone in the Universe. The imp said that, like all imps, it came from a large family and then passed some happy hours listing them all by name and describing in detail how they were related to itself and to one another.

This might have bored anyone else, but Moon enjoyed such family descriptions and loved to hear them set out in the greatest detail. He had another reason for encouraging the imp to speak of familiar homely things – to banish fear.

As to why the imp was alone, it seemed reluctant to say and we can only guess just now. Perhaps this will become clear in due course (or not).

They talked on and at times fell silent as each reflected on their situation. Outwardly at least Moon maintained his general attitude of optimism but the imp was steadily losing hope, slipping back into despair and ever longer silences.

They both slept for long periods. At least kindly sleep kept hunger out of mind and allowed time to pass without more distress for them.

And still, far off, just beyond the reach of Moon's sight, some turmoil was happening as if space itself was boiling and spinning. To a fanciful mind whatever this thing was, it might have been watching them, so closely did it track their movement. Although he saw nothing of this, Moon's unease increased.

Days passed before it seemed they were about to have some rare good fortune in the appearance of what they took to be a small moon orbiting a mysterious and unseen distant planet.

This little body was not just travelling and spinning but at the same time performed astonishing loops and twists and turns accompanied by frequent showers of tiny sparks apparently linked to changes in its speed.

These acrobatics continued throughout their encounter so that

Moon became somewhat light-headed and perhaps just a little less sensible than usual.

{Author's note

No, I cannot tell you the name of either the moon or her planet, nor where they might be found. Celestials generally dislike intrusion into their worlds.

And why should they like it?

Taking and publishing inappropriate photographs is bad enough. Sending spacecraft to land on them and rudely poke about in the name of Science is worse; especially when unkind and insensitive Science dumps piles of untidy space junk to lie about the place for ever and a day.}

Happily, it seemed this little moon was friendly to strangers and quite willing to answer Moon's questions.

"Hail young moon! I am Moon of the Solar System far from here and this is an imp, my colleague and travelling companion. We are very glad to meet you and trust you are well."

"And hail to you, Moon and small being!" Came the reply. *"I am well indeed. Thank you for asking.*

Where, may I ask, is your planet? It doesn't seem to be accompanying you which I imagine is rather awkward for a moon."

And so the conversation proceeded with all the due stodgy formality required of meetings between strangers throughout the polite Universe. Fortunately on the occasion of this meeting, the imp was so subdued by its recent travel experiences that it altogether forgot to put on its pompous act to impress (or annoy) this cheerful little stranger.

"We have become separated from our planet, Earth, and want very much to return to her." Replied Moon. *"It would be appreciated if you would help by telling us where we are. We can't recognise any of the star*

constellations we see around us."

"That" said the young moon *"is because you are looking at stars from here and not from where you would usually look at them. They don't all lie in one plane you know and even if they did, that wouldn't help much."*

Moon stayed silent, annoyed with himself that he had overlooked such an obvious point and afterwards quietly muttering something about parallax. Of course, the appearance of a group of stars would change according to where one stood.

His task, he now realised, must be to identify individual stars and, from their positions, determine their course home. Eventually visible stars would resolve themselves into their familiar patterns as they neared their own dear Sun.

For a moment Moon quite forgot his present situation as he escaped into comforting thoughts of home.

The imp, who had come to view Moon as a friend needing some protection (and what a change that was!) evidently felt that it ought to do something to save the conversation from dying altogether as Moon's embarrassing silence lengthened.

Unfortunately it chose to use its lofty manner which was hardly likely to improve matters:

"Naturally we know all about that, young moon. We hardly expected to see familiar constellations throughout our travels.

What we ask is: can you identify any major stars that we can see from here?

This is just a check you will understand; my friend Moon here is a most excellent and capable navigator and does not really need any information."

The stranger suppressed a smile at this obvious nonsense. But, instead of sailing away without another word, she replied:

"Your friend says you are lost. There is no shame in that; by your appearance you have obviously had a long and troubled journey.

Naturally you need guidance and that is more easily obtained by friendly politeness than pomposity. (Here, to Moon's great amusement the imp lowered its head briefly by way of a rare apology).

Now, if you look upward and to your left, you will see…"

The sparkling little being directed the travellers to the locations of several named, familiar stars before she set off again with a kindly:

"Farewell friends, may the fates be kind to you today and all days hence. Beware of the unknown and trust true friends."

"And may the fates be kind to you today and ever on."

Came the proper reply as the little moon spun and whirled and looped around, accompanied by numerous tiny multi-coloured sparkles of light as she sped away. They never did see her planet and Moon wondered how that could be.

As to her warning, he could make nothing of it, but it naturally worried him. What did she know and why had she not told them what to beware of?

Alone again, the pair looked carefully around their sky and at each of the brightest stars.

For some reason it seemed that neither of them had listened sufficiently carefully to the small moon's advice or maybe that advice had been too vague, even wrong. Perhaps they had both been mesmerised by her. Whatever the reason, they failed to identify any star with certainty.

Moon thought he recognised some of them but the imp was unsure and, where the imp felt confident, Moon was in doubt. In short, they were in as much difficulty as ever in finding their way home.

"I'm beginning to wonder about that moon." said the imp, "Can she be trusted? Was she misleading us? Did you notice that she was spinning the wrong way and she certainly wasn't Titan, the wonky old wobbler?"

"I made the decision to trust her and I shall stick to it. But you're quite right, now that I think about it, she was going the wrong way about, I

wondered what was making my head spin."

"Mm, you were looking a bit giddy, quite moonstruck in fact. I thought you'd fallen for her – love at first sight and all that stuff."

"Nonsense, I've better things to do. But come to think of it, she was very pleasant and extremely moon-like."

Here Moon went quiet for a moment and looked rather wistful.

"Perhaps we shall meet again one day but that doesn't seem likely."

"Well, I'm still not sure she was quite the helpful object she seemed."

And the imp never was sure.

They sailed on despairingly. The imp slept much of the time now and, even when it was awake, seemed to have lost hope and almost all interest in their fate.

But Moon stayed awake much of the time, keeping a hopeful watch for anything familiar that would give him some means to learn where they might be, and still his feeling of unease grew. It had become stronger than ever now, frequently taking over his thoughts; pushing earlier fears into the background.

These strange skies remained a mystery to him and his thoughts turned to their encounter with the small moon. He began to wonder if it really did have a planet far away and out of sight. Somehow, although he was even now in a similar situation, far away from his own dear Earth, that doubt chilled him but for no obvious reason.

A sudden lurch jarred Moon fully awake but left the imp still lost in the safety of its dreams.

Moon scanned the vast volume of space around them. At first

he could see nothing that might have been the cause. More jarring, and suddenly he could see there was something strange and very ominous a long way off to his left, at the furthest reach of his sight.

Again now, they were travelling very fast. Their own small world seemed full of vibration. Whatever Moon had seen, it was closing on them, covering great distances in unbelievably short time.

He saw the mysterious phenomenon in growing detail as it closed on them during the next few hours. Indeed he couldn't take his eyes away from it. Whatever it was, Moon had seen nothing like it before, although it stirred some buried memory, perhaps from mystic tales out of the past or maybe an experience related to him by Sun long ago but now largely forgotten.

One fact was clear: whatever it was, it scared him.

Nearer now, it seemed as if a great volume of space was behaving like a liquid, a huge blackish sea, heaving, boiling and spinning in a great circling eddy. In its centre the sea was sinking, still revolving, a great rounded vortex falling endlessly in apparent slow motion down into a seemingly bottomless pit.

The sense of massive power and violent vibration were overwhelming him, the scale of it all unbelievable. As it travelled this thing was throwing out great fiery jets of material and energy that escaped its surface and reached far out into space. Its gravitational pull was beyond anything he had experienced before.

Moon loved adventures and, like all members of the Solar System, he was naturally brave but now he was lost, frightened, horribly alone. Adventures are fine when you expect the awkward bits to come to a comfortable end and can look forward to telling your envious friends all about them. But facing a hopeless situation far from any help is an altogether different matter.

That requires the greatest bravery of all.

He felt weak and sick. Trembling, he tried to steady himself but his attention was caught by an event that horrified and disgusted him, yet still he could not look away.

A large pale shape appeared, slowly turning at the inner edge of this horrible spinning sea. Shocked, Moon realised it was a small planet complete with its two, now stationary, moons. Unable to stop watching, he saw the thing was lifeless, pale and strangely transparent as if it had been drained of the spirit that once filled it. Yet it seemed to look at him with its dead eyes as if saying *"See me, this will soon happen to you"*.

As he watched, the dead planet was drawn at first slowly, then with increasing speed toward the centre of the thing's nightmare activities. Suddenly their speed increased. Then planet and moons were gone leaving no trace whatever: as if they had never existed. The whole episode had taken no more than an hour and already that boiling sea was much closer.

Freed sufficiently to turn his gaze elsewhere, he saw more sad debris, asteroids, moons, planets all lifeless, turning over and over on the extremities of the vortex, held captive there as if waiting in some inescapable queue for the monster's selection, each to be dragged in turn into its abyss according to some awful plan of systematic destruction.

Against his will, Moon's mind turned to wondering what happened to the victims after they were drawn into the vortex. Whatever he imagined, there was no comfort in the thought.

And, after their destruction, then what? He saw the dark red and dull gold jets of matter and energy spurting up from the thing's surface and thought he knew the answer to that question.

Struck dumb, Moon watched as the destroyer came closer. Here was something way beyond anything he had seen before or even heard of, except in old half-unbelieved legends. This monster was capable of consuming anything and just then Moon and the imp were right in its path.

As if this were not more than enough, drawn by some new enormous force, they lurched in another direction.

Resisting the desire to close his eyes and wait, blindly, for whatever end Fate had arranged for them, Moon looked in the direction of this second disturbance.

Away to his right he saw another darkened space, another vortex, evidence of yet another dreadful power, complete with its own accompanying spinning store of dead beings.

Whatever they might be, there were two of these monstrous things spinning in opposite directions, but travelling together, a dreadful tandem of horror.

Twisting first one way then another, he watched the march of these two super-powerful phenomena, scared beyond any fear he had known before.

For a time it seemed the vortex on his left would reach them first, then he was sure the other, behind, would be the one to capture, then destroy them at its leisure.

Worse still, if worse were possible, he then became convinced they were about to merge into something even larger and more dreadful with the power to swallow anything and, perhaps, everything, no matter what size.

A new object caught his attention; a small, bright body, spinning and flying deliberately across that horrible scene. As it travelled it sparkled and danced.

With its arrival Moon sensed a new force pulling him toward the nearest vortex. He struggled against it, panic overwhelming him as his strength weakened.

But his resistance was futile; there might as well have been an invisible rigid connection between Moon and the sparkling being. There flashed into his mind the idea that it was a servant to powerful masters, bringing prey to them for some unknown, but surely hateful, reward.

Through all his present fears, Moon recalled Sun's advice; whatever happened he must keep resisting - and indeed what else could he have done? He fought down his panic and struggled, fighting a long, lonely and silent battle. But, like someone slipping slowly but inevitably downhill toward a cliff edge, despite all his efforts, he was drawn onward, carrying the unconscious imp with him.

His fight to survive lasted until Moon's strength wavered. His opponent seemed to sense the weakness, suddenly increasing its pull as if celebrating certain victory.

Yet, expecting to be flung straight into the waiting vortex as he lost the last of his strength, Moon found himself yanked violently away in a curved flight, first at a tangent to his previous motion then moving away from that awful place, slowly, then faster as the opposing force weakened with distance.

Moon could hardly believe it. He travelled on, allowing himself time free of all thought for that wonderful feeling of simple relief to fill his mind and being.

After some while he recovered enough to wonder what had happened. Had the sparkling thing suddenly changed its intentions or was it trying to pull him to safety from the start, cleverly planning that curving escape path? Was this an enemy turned friend or had it been true from the beginning when they asked for help?

But then, friendly or not, the rescuing force suddenly ceased. Powerless after his long struggle, Moon realised they were being drawn back toward the vortex.

They hadn't escaped at all.

And now he had no strength to resist.

Whether overwhelmed by exhaustion or shocked into a coma, the imp hadn't moved at all since this fearful episode started.

Glad of only one thing - that his friend knew nothing of what was happening – Moon held the imp tightly to save them from being separated in whatever further violence might come. He closed his eyes and fell, exhausted by fear and physical strain, into a state of blessed unconsciousness.

Time and events passed, as they always will. Whatever happened in the period that followed to that small world of a displaced moon, a young imp and their accompanying little travel case, no-one will ever know; for the only beings that were present were entirely unaware of it all, save for one small spinning body that sparkled and danced as it toiled at its task.

The imp had been awake for some hours.

Unwilling to disturb Moon's deep sleep, it had remained still and silent as they sailed quietly in the light of some kind sun. Still, there was no familiar thing to be seen, no recognisable planet, nor star, nor any known constellation.

When Moon did wake, he found the imp rather more cheerful and a great deal hungrier - a problem that it wasn't slow to complain about. The imp however said nothing about the horrors of so many hours, or days, earlier.

Moon realised with a slight shock that his companion had been entirely unaware of it all and, having no wish to relive the experience himself, he stayed silent. But he could not stop his thoughts.

With a sickening sensation, Moon suddenly recalled their terrifying situation immediately before he fainted. He struggled to understand how they could have escaped to this peaceful place. Surely that small sparkling thing could not have had the strength to save them?

No explanation came to him either then or afterwards, although in later years he often wondered about what occurred that day.

{Author's note

Much later, Moon told the history of their travels to Sun with the imp listening and adding bits that Moon left out. Thus the whole story (or nearly all of it) eventually became known to the three of them; but they said little of it to others and almost nothing at all to fragile Earth.}

They travelled on. Now at last Moon found that he was able to control their direction and, to some extent, their speed.

This naturally helped his confidence but he still had no idea what course to steer. So many events had occurred since they had set out to return to his happy Solar System that for all Moon knew, it was still just as likely that they were travelling away from his home as toward it.

The information provided by the small moon had proved unhelpful and he wondered again if the imp was right. Had she been deliberately confusing them, even leading them toward the dreadful spinning abyss which had so nearly captured them? Could that evil power have its own servants, drawing its victims to it?

He dismissed the idea, recalling that, although she had named some stars, she had not pointed Moon in any particular direction. Nor apparently had she tried to influence their choice of route.

In any case, she seemed so helpful and cheerful that Moon did not want to believe she intended to set them astray. Yet a shadow of that thought and doubt remained.

Disappointed and increasingly tired they drifted on. Both of them dozed, then slept again.

A small bright sparkling thing that had followed them unnoticed came closer. Weaving in its flight it came to a standstill and hovered over the sleeping pair. Without anything done by Moon, their direction of travel changed; their speed steadily increased until they were travelling as fast as they had ever done during their earlier journeys.

Again with no input from Moon, they slowed down by gentle stages as they arrived in some new, but still strange, part of space. Unknowing, they had travelled vast distances since they fell (or were sent) into sleep. Now their direction changed again to follow some new course.

Their sparkling companion drew closer, hovered very close for a brief time, then disappeared.

When Moon awoke, for no particular reason he felt more confident about their prospects but thought how much he would have appreciated guidance from any of his wise friends, especially Sun.

But Sun was far away. A decision had to be made and Moon had to make it, so he decided to keep to their present direction and speed for no better reason than a feeling that all other courses were wrong. As things turned out, it was the right choice.

Having done nothing very much, still exhausted by recent events, Moon promptly fell asleep again and quite naturally dreamt of food - great quantities of it!

A sudden swerving motion jolted both travellers awake. Opening his eyes, Moon saw what looked like a tiny planet with a moon nearly as large as itself nearing them at great speed. They were either about to hit this careless traveller or pass very close.

Nearer now, he recognised the double world of Pluto and Charon.

As you may know, at one time Pluto was described as a planet until some unkind astronomers decided it was not. This was hardly fair on poor Pluto, who feels his downgrading very strongly. He is forever muttering about it along the lines:

> *"I get knocked about by every bit of cosmic rubbish just because I'm not big enough to push it out of the way and as if that isn't bad enough, 'They' use that as an excuse to throw me out of the Planetary Club. I don't even get invited to the annual meetings any more..."*

Complaining and at times weeping a little, Pluto goes on his unhappy way, hardly seeing anything around him and, as you may note from his painfully battered features (although he does have a few smooth areas), he suffers a lot from collisions.

He does, however, have a surprisingly warm heart for reasons that scientists can only guess at, which just shows they don't know everything despite their overbearing belief in themselves. It's enough for us to know simply that it is a good thing to have a warm centre.

Now, as we have seen, Moon has the friendliest of natures and, just as you might expect, he hailed Pluto, first to avoid another nasty collision which neither Moon nor the imp wanted, secondly because Moon liked Pluto and felt sorry for him.

Also of course this was an opportunity to have some friendly and sorely missed communication with a familiar member of the Solar System.

Knowing that Pluto was inclined to be a trifle short tempered, Moon was careful to address him with great respect and politeness.

"Hail Pluto! I am so glad to meet a friendly planet such as yourself. I do hope you are well.

Forgive me for mentioning it, Pluto, but you seem very far out of your usual orbit. I trust this is not through some trouble such as we have suffered.

I, or more accurately, we, are a little bit lost on our journey back to Earth. It would be very much appreciated if you would tell us where we are and point us in the right direction."

At first it seemed Pluto wasn't going to answer. Filled with his self-pitying thoughts, for a moment he had quite forgotten Sun's instructions and why he was flying about in some obscure part of the Milky Way, far out his usual orbit.

But Pluto was flattered by Moon's polite address and by being described as a proper planet. Also, although he lives among friends in the Kuiper belt and even has moons of his own, he likes a change of company (don't we all). Having a lot of little Plutinos fussing around is pleasing but it can also be tiring.

"Good day Moon. I am pleased to see you well. Sadly I am not, but you won't want to hear about me, as of course, I don't matter.

You have a companion that I don't recognise and I don't much like the look of it. I trust it isn't some sort of troublemaker - we have quite enough of them in the Universe already as I know from bitter experience.

Who or what is it?"

The imp thought this rather pompous speech was very rude coming from a minor planet and wasn't going to let it go without setting things straight:

"I, my good minor planet (or should I call you dwarf?), am an imp of considerable importance. I am making a journey with my friend and it is not for trivial bits of the Solar System to obstruct or delay us, so please be about your business and let us get on our way without more empty chit chat."

A silence deeper than a black hole followed and for a moment it seemed that the Universe stopped all business to listen in and see how this promising encounter was going to develop.

But just then the imp, which had been rummaging for something in Moon's near-empty case was overcome by a fit of sneezing so violent that it covered itself from top to bottom with food debris, reappearing out of the resultant white dust cloud as a sort of imp phantom.

No one could have seen this sight and kept a straight face.

Despite his troubles, Pluto has never quite lost the sense of humour that all planets have. He burst out laughing and, with his ready humour, Moon, of course, did the same. The imp first glared at its companions, then turned its back on them to hide a smile, finally exploding into gales of glorious laughter.

The Universe took a deep breath and returned to its interrupted business of rushing, pushing and rudely colliding as if it were a busy railway station on a Friday at going home time. Once again good humour had worked its happy magic.

Pluto recovered his breath:

"I thank you, little imp, the last time I laughed like that was when Mars set himself alight and had to be smothered at the annual All-comers Bowls Match. Served him right too, the old troublemaker."

For a while at least, that was the end of the imp's pomposity:

"I may have been a little lofty when I spoke just now, Pluto. What I meant to say is: any help you give us would be much appreciated.

I ought also to mention that Moon - who is a rather excessive eater even when he is at home - is constantly demanding food, having by now scoffed everything that we brought with us for our trip.

If you could suggest where we might find a good round meal or three (for my friend Moon, you understand), I should be most grateful."

We are getting to know and understand the imp better now. It is not in imps' natures to take responsibility for anything they can shuffle onto someone else. The imp was hungry too and had been just as keen to find a meal as Moon and, whilst Moon enjoys his food, he certainly isn't "a rather excessive eater".

If you care to look back into an earlier chapter, you will find a short list of his daily meals routine. You must surely agree it is very modest and certainly no more than anyone might need to keep in proper circular shape, especially someone who has a lot of work to do.

Had the dust and crumbs episode not happened, Pluto might have sailed on his forgetful way at this point without bothering further about the travellers or their needs, but laughter uplifts us all, and he replied:

"Imp, I know Moon very well, indeed better than you seem to.

His appetite is not excessive nor have I ever known him to eat excessively or to "scoff" - as you so crudely put it - all the food to hand leaving his companions to go hungry. He is far too good a fellow."

And, having been reminded by Charon why he was off-orbit and what he was supposed to be doing (which was certainly not wandering about with his eyes shut and fretting about his status), Pluto said, with some considerable pride:

"You asked why I am out here in the middle of nowhere, Moon.

The reason is that Sun has commissioned me (of all the planets and moons she might have entrusted with the task) to search for you, Moon, after your peculiar and foolish disappearance.

And, here I am, come to your rescue."

It was a great relief to Moon to hear this and, as he saw that the imp was about to make some further not-so-clever retort to Pluto's little lecture, he quickly - and politely - replied:

"We thank you for your help dear friend. Please let us know if there's anything we might do for you in return when we get home. I can assure you nothing will be too much trouble."

As Moon finished this somewhat risky speech, he smartly tweaked the imp's left ear by way of indicating that any more clever dick comments would not be tolerated from that quarter. Surprisingly the imp took the hint and stayed quiet. (Yes, I agree, thank goodness indeed. It looked at one time as if Moon's companion was going to talk them both into a black hole).

"I thank you, dear Moon, I ask only that, if and when you get home to our beloved Solar system, you do what you can to have me better known and respected as a planet. I'm really very interesting, you know. - Mr Tombaugh should be remembered and honoured."

Well, not yet having thought what this request might entail and despite never having heard the name Tombaugh, this sounded easy enough, so Moon cheerfully replied:

"Of course we shall do what we may for you. I'm sure we can help."

And, little as it may seem, this vague undertaking on Moon's part apparently satisfied Pluto, although very soon afterwards Moon was wondering what, if anything, he might do to aid the little planet's case. As ever he could think of no-one, save Sun, to ask for help and advice in this strange and novel task.

Pluto is a great traveller and knows as much about the visible stars and their constellations as any other body in the Solar System. He is rather proud of this and, in his grumpy way, he was secretly pleased to help Moon and show off his knowledge at the same time.

He pointed out and named many of the visible bright stars, running through the alphabet from Aldebaran, the bull's red eye, through to Vega, the brilliant one.

Moon was both astonished and cheered to find they were

now far closer to home than he had thought. It seemed they had become so used to seeing nothing familiar in their travels, they had failed to recognise familiar stars when they at last appeared.

Although neither Moon nor the imp could remember one half of the stars Pluto named for them, far fewer than half would still have been enough to find their position in space and so plot a course home.

Pluto also told them where, on their journey, they would find steady forces that might help them on their route in much the same way that sailing ships once used predictable trade winds to cross and recross the oceans on Earth's surface.

Then the little planet sprang a small but, as it later turned out, welcome, surprise:

"You may also be interested in something that landed on me when I passed through a mass of mostly Earth originated rubbish.

Despite being a planet, (here Pluto glared at the imp as if challenging it to say anything), *being of modest size, I couldn't help colliding with it."*

He produced a circular container, about the size of a small travelling case, very dented, dusty and scarred. Instantly Moon recognised his box of unwanted presents which had elected to share his journey in place of his nice round case and its far more useful contents.

Astonished, Moon said:

"I regret, dear Pluto the box is mine and it saddens me to think you were obliged to collide with it (or the other way about). I trust your injuries were not serious. It came with me on my journey and at some point I'm afraid I lost it."

"You had better have it then. You need feel no regret on my account. Another impact injury more or less is nothing to me compared with the convenience of others in disposing of their rubbish."

Feeling both irritated and guilty on hearing this, Moon took the troublesome box and passed it to the imp for safekeeping.

"Thank you dear Pluto. I'm very pleased to have met you; your advice has been more welcome than I can say. It will be my pleasure to help as you asked, if I am able to do so.

I wish you farewell and a fine clear path wherever you orbit."

And from the imp:

"That goes for me too, Pluto. You are a fine planet indeed; if anyone says otherwise in my hearing, they will regret it."

"Thank you" replied the little planet, *"I wish you both a trouble-free end to your journey and, imp, please do not get into any battles on my account; I do not want to hear you have been injured!"*

So they parted with far better goodwill between them than at one time seemed possible.

Our wandering travellers moved off at a modest speed, steering for home with more confidence than ever before. After some days they sensed the helpful forces that had been foretold by Pluto but these were not strong and Moon remained in full control of their flight.

Recovering his lost confidence, Moon recognised more stars and, eventually, familiar constellations with none of his earlier doubts. How welcome it was to feel a sense of belonging!

He recalled the dream-given advice to have confidence in himself. With that memory came a strong sense that they were being watched over. This time the feeling raised no fears; he was sure they were being both guided and guarded.

As if his mind had been prodded by some friendly spirit, his thoughts turned to Pluto and the astonishing reappearance of his lost luggage.

"Imp, we may as well open my old box. It might hold something useful,

but I doubt it. Just Christmas and birthday gifts that make the rounds over the years."

The imp was very fond of presents, most of all when they were given to it but other people's were a good second best. It had the box open before Moon had realised that it was locked and that he had no key!

It wasn't the disappointment he had expected.

Rummaging through this odd collection of unwanted gifts from clothing that didn't fit to curious implements of no obvious purpose, they found these aging presents happily included some things to eat. First there was a huge cake made by his bad-cook-cousin, Miranda. Next the imp discovered some extremely stale currant buns from an unknown well-wisher who had plainly been very short of dried fruit when making them.

A feast at home with his old friends could not have thrilled Moon more. The two of them laughed and ate together as they had not done before – and I am happy to say that both humour and (better) food were to figure largely in their future friendship, and do so to this day.

Despite its curious blend of burnt outer and uncooked inner and the inclusion of a teaspoon (which was discovered just in time), the cake was eaten in its entirety. The imp declined the two year old buns; Moon did not but regretted his decision later.

In the old sailing ship days, now sadly past, when navigation was more of a lottery than a science, sailors would greet a successful landfall with huge relief, a glass or two of rum and probably some slight and cynical praise for their captain.

If, on the other hand, they found themselves in Java when the crew had been led to expect Liverpool, the captain could expect the usual hoots of derision and an invitation to *"try again, you old fool"* or some such words of encouragement.

It is said that, if the ship made three successive bad landfalls, the crew would throw their captain overboard and elect a new, but understandably reluctant, leader.

For this reason it's a wise captain that keeps all options open and never tells the crew where they are going until they arrive. By this simple means every landfall may be claimed a success. - At least until cannibals appear on the beach.

Perhaps life has not really changed as much as we think. When Moon became sure that the distant star he had been watching for some time was really his wonderful friend, Sun, and not another mirage, for no reason that he could explain he shouted *"Land-Ho! Fine on the port bow!"* and had no idea where the words came from, or quite what he had meant by them.

Stranger still, the imp seemed to accept this odd outburst with a full understanding as if it were a perfectly natural way of announcing a successful homecoming.

Just as only two planets had noted Moon's troubled departure, so Saturn and Mars alone noted his return. Glad and much relieved to see him back, both greeted his arrival enthusiastically: Saturn with a cheerful wave and her warm dreamy smile, Mars with a great shout and salute of joy.

Their transition into Moon's orbit was achieved without disturbing Earth, who remained fast asleep under Sun's protective influence.

But it was, of course a completely different matter with Sun. Seeing them, she shouted a loud cry of welcome and burst into her full brilliant self with even more warmth than usual.

Still Earth slept on as Moon finished his night time orbit and came at last to his home with the imp.

They found news of their return had gone ahead of them thanks to Saturn (who is the chief gossip of the Solar System) and Mars (who never can keep silent about anything that excites him).

A kindly being had stocked Moon's empty food cupboards and set a generous meal on his circular table. The friends ate, then bathed away some of the dust and grime of travel, although it was days before either of them felt completely clean.

Yet there remained invisible stains from their travels, both good and bad, that could not be washed away. These will remain with them both, as you might expect, for the rest of their lives.

So must all great events in life leave their mark on us. As they should. For, if they did not, we should all be very uninteresting both to others and to ourselves.

Then at last Moon rolled gratefully into his bed and the imp wrapped itself up in the soft blankets of Moon's guest suite which was to be its luxurious home for quite some time to come.

Both slept the sleep of exhaustion and relief. For once this was sleep untroubled by dreams of any sort, at least as far as we know.

Chapter 9

Friends, food and familiar things

After turmoil and travel, what better than home and feast? Another adventure maybe, but not just yet!

You might have thought that on the following night Moon would have slept on well after his proper time for getting up. This was not the case. Old habits stay in control of our day to day lives and Moon had his timetable to follow.

On this, his first night home, he had more than his usual tasks to do. Far from having a lunar lie-in (that is lingering in bed when, like Moon, one has a night shift to face), he was up and busy much earlier than usual.

There were so many that he wanted to see and just the same number that were quite as eager to welcome him, to hear his adventures and meet the imp, that he felt he would have to spread catching up on his socialising over several weeks, if not months. And so it proved.

But he was not going to delay meeting Mother Earth, the gentle sleeper.

He was unsure how to handle this. Earth was easily upset, always worrying about others and quite wrongly fearing that the worst had happened when most often it had not. If Earth did not even know he had been away, Moon would have to break that rather old news to her and take things as they came.

Not expecting the imp to be awake, Moon was preparing to set out alone for this meeting when his friend appeared, not just awake but keen to accompany him and meet everyone.

Imagining how it would be if the imp was its worst (that is, rudest) self when meeting his loved ones, Moon tried to think how he might at least delay an encounter with Earth.

It is said that telling the truth is always best, so Moon tried rehearsing something along the lines:

"Imp, please take note that today I shall be visiting Mother Earth who is much loved but very sensitive. We all take care not to upset her. If you come with me, you will probably be pompous and rude as you generally are with strangers and you will distress her.

So please stay here.

What is more, as I don't want any of my other friends to be offended either, please do not answer the door to callers."

Although a perfectly honest approach, Moon felt this ought perhaps to be put in kindlier words. But while he was thinking this over and trying out various alternative speeches in his mind, he found he was saying out loud something quite different from his intention:

"Imp, I'm so pleased you want to come, it will be wonderful to have you along. Earth and any others we may happen to see will be delighted to meet you. They are all my friends and will certainly become yours.

Just be prepared for a good deal of eating."

The imp seemed quite happy to hear this unintended invitation but not as if it was unexpected and Moon found himself wondering, not for the first time, if the imp had some power of control over what others said. A power which it used whenever it wanted to defeat probable objections before they were voiced.

As the imp was used to having breakfast at the start of a day with dinner and supper at its end, Moon's inside out life was quite confusing but whether it was breakfast or a supper, the meal they ate before leaving on their social tour was both substantial and satisfying to it. Moon on the other hand did not think so:

"I'm sorry there was so little, I can only apologise for the limited amount

of food in my cupboards and the want of variety – a mere three sorts of cake (and not one of them chocolate) is a disgrace on the part of any host.

We shall have to hope that miserable meal will keep us in round form until we get there; Earth generally knows how to entertain, provided she isn't asleep (which is all too likely)."

Having lived until then with absolutely no consideration for others, except as targets for practical jokes, the imp was finding the Solar System difficult to understand.

Hardly ever having made any genuine apology itself and, unsurprisingly, having acquired no friends, Moon's world seemed alien but at the same time something to be envied rather than despised.

And the encounter with Earth was not what the imp expected at all.

Privately the words "downright weird" went through its mind at their first meeting and, for once in its life, it blushed in embarrassment as Earth gave a sad, even tearful, look which showed she had read the unspoken thought. Such is the power of so many celestials – it can be unwise and even cruel to think careless thoughts.

Her visitors had found Earth half asleep (that is to say a good deal less dormant than Moon had expected).

Once she was sufficiently awake to recognise that she had guests and that one was her moon, Earth greeted him with her natural generous warmth but she did not seem either surprised to see him or even conscious that he had been absent for any length of time.

"My dearest, it's so good to see you. Please introduce your friend and let it tell me all about itself."

Fearing what the imp might say and in consequence feeling as if he had just eaten a two year old bun, Moon thought of pretending the imp was nothing to do with him and had hitched a ride unnoticed but he rejected such a story as being impossible to keep up for long. If he took that course, the imp would certainly take delight in tripping him up at the worst possible moment.

"This is where it all goes wrong" thought Moon but what he said was:

> *"This, dearest Earth, is my friend. It is an imp. We have travelled a long way together and shared some surprising adventures, but nothing dangerous or worrying. In fact on reflection it has all been quite boring.*
>
> *That's enough of us. Do tell me how you are keeping and what is your own news."*

This was Moon carefully telling nothing at all about the imp's troublemaking and as little as possible about their frightening experiences, so he was quietly pleased when Earth seemed not to pick up on the words *"surprising adventures"*. In fact for one moment he thought she might have fallen asleep (yet again) and was considering slipping away, taking the imp with him, when she said in her gentle way:

> *"I am so happy to meet you dear Imp. I hope you had sufficient food when you were away.*
>
> *I always worry that Moon doesn't look after himself as he should. Sometimes he seems quite transparent – it's all that nightwork, you know – and then I just have to insist he has a few extra meals before he does anything else."*

The imp, who had already fallen under Earth's kindly spell, was (unusually) determined not to upset her in any way. Far from putting on the pompous-with-strangers act, following Moon's example, it answered in carefully chosen words:

> *"Thank you for your welcome dear Earth (if I may call you so). I'm delighted to meet you, too.*

Yes, there were times on our journeys when we were a little short of lunches and suppers but it was nothing to trouble us really."

(Here Moon broke into a bout of coughing which the others politely pretended not to notice).

"And," the imp continued, glaring at Moon, *"we have eaten very well since our return."*

"Well," said Earth, *"I'm glad to hear it was all a pleasant holiday for you both. Now you must have a breakfast, or is it supper for you Moon? Your timetable always confuses me."*

"After breakfast-breakfast would be about right Earth but please don't trouble to cook for us." said Moon.

Moon thought if they accepted Earth's offer in her present dozy state, the meal was likely to be a sad disappointment unless she had a sudden (and very unusual) bout of wakefulness. Making breakfast whilst wearing only your nightclothes is all very well - unless hot sausages fall in an awkward place - but few can cook a decent meal while staying fast asleep.

Happily, Moon (who you will remember was disappointed in his earlier breakfast and still hungry) need not have worried.

Earth did produce a meal (substantial by most standards but still on the slim size for Moon) although how the sleepy old planet achieved this remained a mystery until their later meeting with Sun.

After they had eaten, Earth nodded off into another peaceful doze. Seizing the moment Moon tried to leave noiselessly but a cheerful *"Goodbye Earth!"* from the imp woke her to say:

"Surely not leaving yet Moon? It's time you had a meal" (here someone made a choking sound). *"Imp, my dear, tell me about your family and how you come to be wandering alone.*

Then I want to hear all about your recent travels with Moon. I hope he looked after and protected you — you seem so very young."

This was just what Moon didn't want but before he could stop it, the imp was replying.

As ever, it said nothing of its family but chattered cheerfully about adventures with Moon, meetings with other moons and planets, getting lost and finding their way home but said almost nothing of the violence and fears of their travels and so, happily, gave Earth no cause for alarm.

As the imp talked, Moon and Earth listened with kindly tolerance as if a much-loved child might have been speaking of its imaginary adventures and, as they listened, so their fondness for this small outcast grew.

To Moon's relief nothing was said about pyjamas or practical jokes or even upsetting hard working smugglers. Perhaps Earth never learned any of this, or maybe she did but was too polite to show it. I am inclined to believe it was the latter; despite her dreaminess, Earth misses little.

When the imp's flow of chatter halted to accommodate a cream cake, Moon took the opportunity. Taking a firm grasp on it, he steered his friend away saying:

"Sorry to rush off dear Earth. We have to ..."

But Earth was back to sleep again and did not even know they had left.

Sun, who was next on their visiting list, had been busy since she heard of Moon's return. She was, of course, responsible for the food in Moon's home, for the meal just enjoyed with Earth and a host of tasks done in organising the inevitable forthcoming "Hooray-he's-home" celebration feast.

That isn't to say no-one else was involved or helped in any of these kindly tasks but nothing would have been achieved without her. On their own, her "helpers" would have expended all their time discussing either menus or recent Bowls matches. As we have seen, they are an absolute liability when gathered together.

Moon was already late for his night's work but reunion with Sun was more important to him than anything.

It was a joyful meeting between these two great friends. At first the imp felt rather unwanted and ignored but no-one can be in Sun's boisterous presence without being uplifted.

Although completely different from Earth, each of them made the imp feel that here was a world of easy, generous friendship and warmth unlike anything it had known. Quite simply it longed to be a part of it as Sun welcomed him:

"Imp, I'm delighted to meet you at last. I know you were a great aid and comfort to Moon on your travels together.

No! I don't want to hear every detail. I travelled with both of you in my dreams and gave you what help I could along your way, although you may not have known it.

Now isn't the time to relive the past – that can take care of itself without our help. Your next task is to celebrate with a cheerful meal, just the three of us together. Then you can tell me what you think of my plans for a grand feast."

While Sun was busy preparing food, the imp was wondering just how much they were all going to eat in one day and worrying about what she meant by travelling with them on their journey. – How much did Sun know? Did this include all the troublemaking, starting with Moon's irritating nightwear for instance? Then how had Sun aided them? What dreams was she talking about?

The imp noticed that Moon was looking on with a slight smile of amusement, leaving it even more puzzled and a little worried about what was coming next in this strange company but Moon just said:

"Don't worry Imp. Sun knows much but not all. She would be just the same wonderful caring and uncaring being if she did know everything; loving her entire Solar System always, whatever its faults.

When you're with her, it's best to sit back and enjoy life as it comes. You will get plenty of excitement but the right kind."

And the imp had to be satisfied with that, for neither of these strange but likeable companions made any further reference to the recent past. Whatever they knew of its impish mischief-making, they kept to themselves not just at that moment but for all time. That was their kindly way.

No more need be said about this first meeting of three who were to become fast friends, save for two points.

First, Sun's promise of a "cheerful meal" was, of course, thoroughly fulfilled (and they were all filled full by it).

Secondly, Sun and Moon talked of the game of Bowls (or Planetary Bowls to give its full title) as if it were a far more important subject than all their recent experiences in space from meetings with other worlds to escapes from fearsome black holes.

The imp wanted to know more about a game that so absorbed its friends and, once Sun was convinced the imp was not merely being polite, she embarked on an explanation of the game with practical illustrations that involved some violent impacts with her furniture and several newly singed areas in her huge carpet.

To the imp, Sun's description was a call to play this exciting game; it appealed strongly to its practical joking spirit and we shall see later how Bowls became a central part of its life just as it had taken its hold on both Sun and Moon.

There is little about Sun's grand reunion celebration day that you will not be able to imagine perfectly well for yourself.

It is sufficient to say that everybody able to attend did so. A vast amount of food was consumed; Moon was for once prepared to admit that he could eat no more (at least until the next meal); the imp forgot to be pompous and the numerous speeches were satisfyingly dreary, allowing everyone else to talk loudly over the speechmakers without the least embarrassment.

The imp did make a speech but the cheers and heckling were

so loud, no-one, including the imp, heard a word of it. Knowing how its tongue can run away, this may have been a good thing or it may not; we shall never know.

{In answer to a couple of questions:

Yes, Earth was of course present and (unusually) awake. She, talked very happily to her neighbour, Saturn, mostly about her wonderful Moon and, in return, patiently hearing Saturn's near-endless descriptions of the activities of her own numerous satellites of whatever size.

At the end of the party these two both went home to catch up on their sleep, well pleased with the day and totally forgetful of everything the other had said.

And, what happened to the many and various celestial bodies that were unable to attend through force of circumstances? For of course no-one actually wished to miss any well-fed occasion.

Of those we have met, only Io and Pluto were absent; Io was recovering from a severe bout of breathlessness on account of a particularly violent squeezing session by her careless family and Pluto, together with his five moons, was simply too far away and grumpily travelling in the wrong direction.

Many others, too numerous to name, also missed out. However, whether they had been likely to come or not, generous Sun had made sure all were invited to her homecoming feast and for those who could not be there, she sent to each a personal gift and a token morsel of "Friendship Cake", of which we may learn more later, or perhaps not.}

Just as the welcome home feast marked the end (for the time being) of Moon and the imp's foreign adventures, it also saw the start of recovery and repair in the Solar System of the many things that had gone wrong during the Great Disappearance.

Earth was aware of the widespread unhappiness among people living on her surface even though she didn't know the cause: Sun's protection had been effective in sparing her that.

Much concerned for her troubled people, Earth asked Sun what could be done to help them but she got only a typical Sun reply:

"Don't worry Earth, just leave that problem to me and have a nice sleep for a couple of months while I attend to it."

Confirming what Moon had long suspected (that Sun could put Earth to sleep at any time and for pretty much as long as she wished), Earth promptly fell asleep and stayed that way for rather longer than Sun had intended. But her dreams, largely concerning Moon when he was very young, were very pleasant so we need not worry too much about that.

Sun was well aware of the trouble on Earth and much regretted her unintended part in it. The blue planet had been denied a large part of her usual radiance and, as we have all seen, even a slight increase or reduction in darkness and cold may be harmful to living beings. All life depends on its regular ration of energy.

Within a surprisingly short time after Moon's return, Earth's ocean tides had recovered their regularity and scale. But the effects of past shortfalls in Sun's warmth and light took longer to make good. She could not speed things up by substantially increasing her radiance without risking further, but different, damage.

So she raised her brilliance very slightly and began by clearing the depressing mists over Earth's surface.

The effect on Life was immediate. Sunshine always cheers, especially when it's been missed for a long time. People were not just warmed but, more importantly, uplifted as they welcomed the first positive change in weather since Moon's disappearance.

With the mists cleared, people were less fearful and life became a little easier, although there was a long way to go before Sun's warmth returned everything to normal.

Some however were quick to get back to their old ways.

Burglars, now having the benefit of dark nights and predictable moonlight to help their labours, set about making up for lost time by working double shifts and burgling faster than ever before.

Indeed, within the first month of Moon's return the records for the number of houses emptied of their contents and for country mansions stripped of their lead roofs in a single night were both broken three times.

These feats could hardly be maintained for long. Several thieves had to be treated for exhaustion and given long periods of bed rest before doctors certified their fitness to return to work with strict instructions to avoid using heavy ladders and to take weekends off in future.

As for grave robbers, there were was a massive backlog of work and so much to do that it was impossible to recruit enough people to meet the need for them.

Matters became so serious that, even with robbers daringly working during the day as well as night, many graves simply remained unexcavated. The general standard of workmanship became most unsatisfactory; empty coffins and piles of soil were left lying about beside open holes and the lack of safety in churchyards was an international disgrace.

The situation was eventually improved by governments introducing heavy taxes on dying (now referred to as Inheritance Tax) and thereby reducing the burden of work in the body disposal industry.

As Sun continued to bathe Earth (and all others within the Solar System) in generous warmth and light, so temperatures rose and more aspects of life returned to their familiar and welcome state.

People began to realise that sunny holidays were possible, first in countries close to Earth's equator, then gradually moving further away North and South toward the Mediterranean, then to Australia, in due course even the English Riviera and eventually sunny Scunthorpe. Skiing returned to its proper locations. Cruising regained its attractions once the chances of one's ship being frozen in for the duration of a boring holiday became less likely.

Unfortunately, Sun, being her usual over-enthusiastic self and inattentively thinking too often about cookery matters, went just a little too far with her solar heating, causing sea levels on Earth to rise alarmingly, burning more than the usual number of careless holiday-makers bright red and melting a lot of igloos to the distress of Inuit families who watched their comfy homes dissolve into useless puddles.

Luckily Moon spotted what was happening before matters got completely out of hand. Sun made some urgent corrections and Earth was saved from waking up to find she had changed in her sleep from a watery blue planet to a dry orange one.

As we saw earlier, the loss of tides had distressed some people as much as Sun's waning strength. Moon now being back in his proper orbit, tides returned, happily occurring in their predictable amounts and at their due times. With sea levels and tides back to normal, seafarers were returned to a world they understood.

There were no more embarrassing situations for naval officers marooned on their grounded ships. Small boys went back to catching revolting things from seaside piers. Smugglers returned to their tasks with renewed enthusiasm and revenue men were delighted to have them back.

So quite soon all was as well and normal as it ever can be on Earth with human beings about the place. There remained however a faint shadow of doubt for, if Moon had disappeared once without warning and with such terrible consequences, could he not vanish again in the future?

On this point, scientists made no clear prediction.

Some, having supported the *"Moon isn't a moon and therefore did not exist and could not have disappeared"* argument were absolutely consistent in saying *"No comment"* whenever they were careless enough to be caught in public by television reporters.

Other astronomers were more inclined to respond to questions with a firm *"We are looking into it"*, thereby ensuring that their government grants for the Moon Disappearance Research Project continued for a further year or so.

It is unsurprising that, by now, a great many among Earth's populations had lost faith in scientific "explanations" for unusual happenings in the Solar System.

Disappointed by discredited science, some people grew to believe that Moon's temporary disappearance and Sun's coolness were indications of celestial displeasure for not being treated with sufficient respect in recent times.

Of course, we now know that was wrong but, once a thought takes root, it may grow vigorously and so it was in this case. The idea that Sun, Moon and indeed all celestial bodies ought to be respected and valued soon gathered a substantial following even to the extent that some reverted to the ancient practice of openly worshipping them.

Although, happily, this fell short of slightly naughty practices like sacrificing troublesome neighbours at midnight, devotional sects appeared in every country on Earth. Mostly they worshipped by offering gifts of round chocolate cakes on weird circular shrines and chanting equally weird nonsense in praise of anything that appeared in the night (or day) sky.

Such practices didn't last long as they led to a number of silly and well-publicised mistakes. These included the several occasions when groups of devotees were found to have been singing hymns to passenger planes and man-made communication satellites. And, of course there was the odd episode involving the racing pigeon and a drunken farmer.

However the belief that the rest of the Universe, or at least what we can see of it, ought to be respected and not ignored remained undiminished. And why not?

Although Sun and her family were pleased but largely unaffected by changing attitudes on Earth's surface, for one of them the effect was positive and cheering.

Seizing an opportunity to benefit from this general goodwill, the "Friends of Planet Pluto" (or "**FOPP**" as it is commonly called) renewed their crusade to have Pluto reinstated to full planetary status.

So, Moon need not have worried about how he could help Pluto's case. Without knowing it, both he and the imp were already unintentionally doing just that when they met the small planet and listened to his sad complaint in their chance meeting far from home.

Chapter 10

Bowls and practical jokes

***No friends are so close as those that
have shared both hardship and joy.***

Back home, the two friends settled into the orderly life of Sun's Solar System.

The imp was now well and very happily settled into Moon's guest rooms. At first their size and luxury had been rather overwhelming but it was all so very comfortable that any feeling of awe soon gave way to easy acceptance as it became a much-loved permanent home.

Moon sailed the night skies, following his phases as he had always done. Sun shone warmly on everyone according to her own timetable. Earth caught up on her missed sleep (yes, really!) and Imp (for so we may call him since he has now matured and aged well beyond the stage of being just 'the imp') spent some of his time with Sun and more of it with Moon.

But he did not neglect any of his new friends, especially Earth and her people for whom he had a special fondness.

In fact he was most welcome wherever he went, not least on account of his great liking for all types of amusement, especially Planetary Bowls.

Imp had a natural talent for this celestial game. When Moon took him to his first match (just to watch and understand it) Imp immediately wanted so much to play that Moon had him included in the next second division all-comers asteroids match as a member of the local Rocky Fragments team.

Playing in this game for the first time ever, Imp distinguished himself by scoring two Halleys despite being rolled on twice by a small ice covered moon and scorched by a careless visiting comet from his own team.

From then on, apart from one incident that we shall come to later, Imp's rise into the top division was meteoric and he became a leading advocate of the game's benefits to health and goodwill throughout the Solar System and beyond.

{Historical footnote:
How Rules for Planetary Bowls came to be written

You will be surprised and, hopefully, impressed to know that it was Imp who devised a formal set of rules by which the game came of age. These were to become the *"Common Regulations for Planetary Bowls Matches"* and used throughout the Solar System where, as you may know, it is played professionally in the three divisions of the Cosmic Bowls League.

In its early days, the full two day game of Bowls (which is divided into twelve four hour "Ursas") was played by much of the Solar System with just two rules: first, all players must spend ninety minutes bumping into as many others as possible whilst endeavouring to score "Halleys" by speeding between the goal posts and shrieking with laughter; the second rule required each player to cause as much laughter as the others could bear without choking.

At the end of each Ursa there would be a two and a half hour refreshment break when everyone rolled indoors to eat as much as possible before the game continued. After all, if you're engaged in a game that depends on rolling about, staying in circular shape is quite important.

In passing, I should add that cheating was encouraged as it helped to keep everyone in good spirits and stopped matters becoming over-serious.

As you may see, from its inception Bowls had a lot in common with football but with the addition of laughter which is of course outlawed by FA regulations. However, unlike that game, Bowls lacked a body of written rules, whereas football, in contrast, has rather too many regulations for comfort.

Because he was small, Imp was somewhat disadvantaged when Bowls matches ran wilder than normal.

He had no problem with being scorched by Venus or frozen stiff by Neptune, and being bumped into by a planet made largely of gas was a trifle smelly but otherwise harmless. However, impacts from harder, heavier and less than ethereal bodies were liable to cause painful bruises and leave him stiff for several days.

Imp would never have suggested making new rules just to suit himself. But it was widely accepted that, in a free-for-all game, however much the smaller players cheated, the winner was almost sure to be one of the largest and heaviest planets or Sun herself, although she generally "let" someone else win out of kindness.

To remedy this imbalance a little and to open up the game to other parts of the Milky Way (and hopefully, further afield) it was settled that Imp should draft a proper set of regulations for every team and player to observe, providing it wasn't complicated and contained no more than three paragraphs.

This he did, coming up with the following:

1. *No player is allowed to roll over another less than one tenth its size. Penalty for non-observance; 1 Halley in favour of the flattened player.*

2. *No player may set light to another more than twice in a game. Penalty: 1 Halley to every singed player. Note – accidental ignitions do not count.*

3. *Unconscious players must be removed from the field before the game continues.*

You will note these are of course the founding rules of soccer, a game which hasn't been around for as long as celestial Bowls but which has accumulated numerous further, and largely unnecessary, regulations in its relatively short life.

Although some thought his rules were typical of 'soft' modern times, it was generally considered that Imp had got things about right. From then on, the new rules were faithfully followed (except when they were forgotten in the general excitement of a closely fought contest; which was quite often).

It should be added that Imp gained a great deal of respect here. And of course from a practical point of view, being one of the smallest players himself, under the new rules he had a (slightly) easier time on the field.

Accordingly the beautiful game of Bowls came of age. With the benefit of formal rules, it could be played anywhere by any team and, happily, it continues to flourish strongly with no indication that its popularity will ever lessen.

The game is played openly in the more remote regions of the Universe where evidence of some of the bigger collisions and ignitions in the course of play can be seen from Earth with a good telescope.

However, nowadays, within our Solar System, all Planetary Bowls matches take place out of sight of Earth's surface. This avoids attracting unwanted attention from silly nosey parkers who have nothing better to do than make a nuisance of themselves by prying into private activities and writing to newspapers or on social media sites about their so-called "findings".}

For the following years Imp continued to live with, and among, Moon and their mutual friends. He enjoyed playing rather too frequent practical jokes on others (although he was just a little less amused when any were played on him) and he never quite lost the unfortunate habit of becoming pompous when addressed by strangers.

In both these matters, Moon did his kindly best to alter his friend's ways but imps are what they are and cannot be wholly changed. Besides, Moon was more inclined to be amused than offended by practical jokes and by cheeky impudence because Imp was now a very good friend and friends are a lot more important than perfect manners.

But Moon was obliged to deal sternly with Imp after two of his practical jokes went further than even he could tolerate.

The first occurred at one of the Annual Celestial Body Meetings.

These yearly gatherings are attended by most members of the Solar System above the rank of asteroid. Their purpose is to maintain good relations and stop small arguments developing into outright war. In other words to keep that old pest Mars from falling out with anyone and everybody and generally make sure that he keeps his spear to himself.

At these meetings everyone stands or spins about, according to individual taste, in their allotted positions around the grand Solar Arena (which is normally used for premier Bowls matches). The numerous mind-numbing speeches are largely ignored as the attendees either sleep or chat among themselves.

At the close of the speeches (that is before the start of the Grand Feast which is the highlight of an otherwise boring day), complete silence is required for the Chairman's Closing Address.

On the occasion I am telling you about, the Chairman for that year was Callisto, representing Jupiter who was absent on account of a serious gas problem. Callisto is of course much revered on account of his age, if not his looks and, although no-one can ever make out what he is saying, all stay very quiet whenever he makes a speech out of deference to the old chap.

So silence duly fell but, before Callisto could start his rambling speech, a high pitched voice screamed

"Watch out Cally, - Black hole behind you!"

Now, except for appalling events like a shortage of toast and tea at breakfast, there is nothing a celestial body fears more than the dreadful words black hole. After a few milli-seconds of horrified quiet, the Solar Arena was almost completely empty save for a strong smell of burning. I say almost because there remained just Moon and, popping up from nowhere, Imp.

Fortunately, most saw the funny side but it took a great deal of time and diplomacy on Moon's part to smooth the ruffled feelings of the crabby ones who persisted in remaining offended.

By way of punishment, Imp was required to apologise separately to everyone who had been present on that day.

His most dreaded meetings were with Mars and Uranus. Uranus gave him a very frosty reception but melted a little when Imp politely admired the antics of Uranus' eccentric family of moons. Eventually they parted on quite good terms after falling into a long discussion about the current Bowls league tables.

No meeting with Mars can be relied on to be easy and Imp would have avoided this one if he could have done. Moon, however, was determined Imp should be made to suffer for his conduct. Mars must be faced.

But, when the time came, the event was less painful than the worry that went before.

That's often the case, isn't it?

You spend a week worrying about seeing your dentist and fearing all sorts of horrid drillings and scrapings. Then, after a fearful lot of poking about in your mouth and tut tutting, you hear the magic words: *"That's all fine; see you in six months."* – The resulting feeling of relief as you race for the surgery door is where the term 'walking on air' comes from.

So it was with Imp and Mars.

Having worried himself sick (and some would say, serve him right), Imp found the old warrior in a rare good mood and quite ready to see the humour in the "Black Hole" episode. This was not least because a couple of small moons that had annoyed Mars in the Annual Meeting by their childish behaviour had fallen over each other and caught light in their haste to escape a non-existent black hole.

So Imp left with no more than a pretend fierce look from Mars and a kindly given case of wine for him to share with Moon.

Imp's second misplaced prank happened on a more domestic level, in fact at Sun's home.

It was the friends' habit for Sun, Moon, Earth and Imp to meet at Sun's vast home once each lunar month for a good lunch – a meal that merged seamlessly through afternoon teas to dinner and even supper, if Sun's larder lasted that long.

On one of these cheerful occasions, Imp arrived earlier than usual bearing a few pies, puddings and pastries sent on ahead from Moon by way of contribution to the meal.

As Sun was busy cooking for her guests, she made a pot of tea for Imp and left him to sit at leisure with a few boxes of biscuits for company in her very large (that is, vast) dining room. There he sat down in one of the new chairs Sun had bought after she had seen (and tried) Moon's wonderfully soothing rocking chair that spun about a room at the sitter's will.

Later, remembering her early guest, Sun looked in to offer a toasted snack and perhaps a cake or two but found the room empty. Imp had gone, and Sun thought no more about it.

Shortly before the time set for the start of their lunch the guests arrived at Sun's home having been a little delayed by a need for a snack before they set out. They had also been tempted on their journey to stop and sample some of the food they had brought with them. As Moon said *"Just to make sure it's up to standard – we don't want anyone to be poisoned."*

And I am pleased to report that it was all to the very highest standard, as you would expect of those excellent cooks Moon and

Earth. Happily, no-one was poisoned, although other things didn't go as smoothly on that day as most of them would have liked.

At first the meal proceeded quite as planned, starting with an assortment of soups. Naturally, they each chose to have every soup on offer in case it might cause offence to refuse a dish that someone else had prepared.

Soup was followed by several more starter courses. After these little snacks, the party moved on to their substantial main dishes, then desserts with several in-between refreshment breaks for coffee and cakes until Sun made the usual announcement at lunch that it was now time to start High Tea.

Naturally there had to be a short interval at this point to allow for the table to be cleared of crockery and empty serving dishes. - There is never anything left uneaten on these occasions, including at times even the tablecloth, as Sun can get carried away when she is eating and talking all at once.

Moon and Earth went to sit in the easy chairs while Imp cleared away and Sun brought out the makings of a massive high tea.

Idly watching these cheerful proceedings and feeling grateful that he had remembered to wear appropriately loose clothing, Moon was surprised to realise that Imp hadn't yet sat down with the others. Instead he was spending a lot of time in Sun's kitchen while frequently peering out from behind the door as if expecting something to happen.

Knowing Imp as he does, Moon felt a slight worry that he was "up to something" but couldn't imagine what. This was a quiet lunch with friends; the cooking was finished, the food was fine, what could go wrong?

There came a whirring sound, at first noticeable only to Moon (although he had no idea what caused it). The noise became louder, rising to a high pitched screech that claimed everyone's attention, save for Imp who remained apparently deaf and busy about something in the nearby kitchen.

It seemed to Moon however that, viewed from behind, Imp was shaking.

The air around them filled with blue smoke. Without warning, Moon's chair began to move, rolling forward on its large wheels, speeding up and at the same time slowly rotating.

The noise grew even louder, roaring now, sparks and bright orange flames accompanied the smoke.

The travelling and spinning motions grew more violent. In no time at all Moon and his chair were whizzing along whilst spinning like a mad planet.

There was a strong smell of burning chemicals as if Fireworks Night had started in Sun's living room. Sun dashed after the racing Moon, Earth fainted (or fell asleep, one can never be sure which with her). Imp had disappeared.

It is fortunate (unless you had to pay for cleaning or a new carpet) that Sun's home is so very large. Any smaller, and Moon's journey might have ended against a wall with who knows what consequences. As it turned out the rocket attached to his chair burned itself out and Moon slowed to a stop in the centre of Sun's singed carpet.

The entertainment ended.

Earth woke up, learned from the others (both speaking at once) what had just happened and promptly fell asleep, or fainted.

Then the hunt for Imp began. There was no debate between them about the cause of Moon's "accident"; it bore all the signs of Imp's practical jokes and, as they boringly say in all those tedious detective series, Imp had means, motive and opportunity. Motive in this case being his irresistible desire to enjoy a laugh at the expense of anyone within reach.

Unable to resist seeing the fulfilment of his rocket trick, Imp had stayed close by, watching with delight as Moon careered about on Sun's fine green carpet and although he had hidden himself well by changing his colour to match the floor, as imps frequently do, it didn't take Moon long to spot him.

The culprit was duly brought out into the open and stood in

front of his friends like a prisoner on trial for misdeeds.

It would be wrong to say that Moon, or for that matter, Sun or Earth, was seriously angry with Imp. It was not in their kindly nature, but they all felt "something had to be done" to stop any more nonsense from their irritating friend.

But none of them had anything to suggest. They could only agree that each would think the matter over before discussing the problem again later. In the meantime, Imp was sent off with nothing more corrective than a black look from Sun, a sad head shaking from Moon and Earth's gentle smile.

The solution was to come from another source altogether.

We noted Imp's enthusiasm for Bowls and how quickly his playing skills developed. He was now playing regularly for Comet Igniters B, a star player in the team. So good in fact that he was being considered for promotion to the A side.

He was told of his likely advancement shortly before the rocket chair incident in Sun's living room but once that tale became generally known (Sun is an awful gossip), the Comet's manager told Imp there was no place in the A team and probably none in any team for someone so irresponsible.

In short, he would be lucky to play again for any side.

This harsh reaction shocked Imp as nothing else could have done, save perhaps having a lighted rocket tied to his chair. He was so obviously distressed and sorry to have made a bad name for himself that he was allowed to stay on as a Comet player. However, he would certainly be sacked if there were any more "incidents".

Imp took the warning to heart and, being the fine player he was, in due course he got his promotion.

The practical jokes did not stop altogether. Indeed, no-one wished him to lose his naughty sense of humour, but from that time onward his tricks were never dangerous or in the least spiteful and his humour was largely directed at himself.

In short Imp had at last grown up.

{Author's apology:

Before we come to the end of this little history, I must apologise for an omission.

Describing our friends' adventures has allowed little room to spare for personal details and you may not have noticed that food and eating are really quite important to all of our characters and all important to quite a lot of them.

It would have been a pleasant task to have described some of their meals in more detail – a typical breakfast for Sun, or maybe the homecoming feast she arranged for Moon (no, that needs a separate book). Perhaps just a light post-supper supper.

Sadly there simply hasn't been the space to give you the thorough detail you deserve. Later perhaps, when we follow Saturn on some of her adventures with Sun, there may be an opportunity to enlarge on the subject, providing that gang of troublesome moons doesn't hog all the attention.

In the meantime, I regret there is neither time nor its close relation, space, to say more on the subject of eating than simply to point to the beautiful roundness of celestial bodies in general which rather speaks for itself.}

Chapter 11

Partings

There is no such thing as final parting from a friend whilst fond memories remain.

Imps are rarely seen nowadays. It is said they are a dying race but I prefer to believe they have just got better at staying out of our sight, or maybe they have largely moved to some more remote part of the Universe.

Whatever the facts may be, our world would be a duller and sadder place without them and their naughty antics.

Such imps as one may now encounter are usually juveniles going through their troublesome growing up period.

Reliable information about imps' domestic lives is rare and hard to come by. They are a secretive lot. However, as I said earlier, it is thought that imp parents send their offspring away at the adolescent stage and welcome them back only when they have matured into tolerable citizens.

This seems to have been the case with our Imp. His time with Moon saw the end of irresponsibility and the beginning of adulthood – well, as responsible and as adult as one may hope for in the case of imps.

So it was that one night, when Moon was sailing across the sky, planning his next meal and idly entertaining himself by suddenly popping out from behind a cloud to illuminate burglars at just the wrong moment, Imp was having his sleep disturbed by strange dreams.

Those dreams would foretell changes. Not all of them would be entirely welcome. But, as we learn through life, time marches on and allows nothing to remain untouched by its passage.

It had been an uneventful day for Imp; partly taken up with helping Sun and Moon to prepare some of their numerous meals and partly in reading the Planetary Times' reports on yesterday's Bowls matches and the sports editor's views on player transfers, team relegations and so on. All much as one might expect from football reporters these days but, of course, a great deal more interesting.

Apart from tying a cardboard pretend rocket to Sun's roll-about chair, Imp had done little physical work but he was unusually tired. It felt as if someone, or something, was weighing him down into sleep.

He was still reading his paper as he went to bed and finished his post-supper supper. You will gather that his eating habits were following his friends' ways and I have to report that his shape was becoming just a little more circular than it ought to be for a youthful imp.

He finished his sandwiches followed by a piece of Earth's special fruit cake, put down his empty cocoa cup and slipped into that half waking, half sleeping state in which reality and dream blur together. It is from there that sleep gently takes over. We enter a world where anything may happen, where distances of both space and time have no relevance and we find ourselves anywhere happily meeting friend or stranger from past or present without need for either effort or explanation.

As he lay there, his bedroom seemed to change; now it was circular, next it was six sided, like a piece of a vast honeycomb and strangely protective, even comforting. It reminded him of something from long ago.

The walls and ceiling became green; slowly the room opened out like a complex cardboard box unfastened, unfolded and laid flat. He stood on a vast sunlit grassy field. As he watched, it filled with wild flowers – violets, yellow buttercups and white daisies.

A stiff breeze set the flowers quivering and combed the grass flat, making it shimmer silver and green. Trees appeared in the distance, waving violently in the wind. The sky was bright blue, populated with small, busy white clouds. A family of crows circled high overhead, joyfully riding the strong eddies and thermals of their private world. It was a day to do things, invigorating and full of promise.

He was aware of something else, some presence, friendly but yet to be seen and fully understood.

The typical sounds of a Bowls match came to him; figures appeared far off. He could not make out what they were but he watched fascinated as they laughed and rolled about; suddenly there came a spurt of flame accompanied by boisterous shouting.

A cloud of smoke hid the scene; sounds faded into distance.

Close by a kindly voice said

"You love the game, don't you?"

For some reason Imp felt that he ought not to see the speaker. Without turning to look he replied:

"Yes. It has helped me in so many ways; growing up, making good friends, being valued…"

Just once more the voice spoke, gently and very quietly

"Then I think you are quite ready, now. We shall expect you one day soon. Take your time and cause no distress in your going."

Then silence. He looked behind him; there was nothing to see; no-one was there. Yet the voice had been so very familiar.

The great grassy area seemed to diminish and fold itself away into the hexagonal box from which it had developed. The blue sky, the wind, the trees, birds and flowers all disappeared. Their dreamer slipped into deeper, now dreamless, sleep.

Later that night, he awoke then immediately fell back into a shallow, near wakeful, doze.

He was standing in the warm, so comforting and familiar,

kitchen with Moon who, in typical Moon fashion, was spreading a large chocolate cake with thick chocolate icing and keeping up a soft flow of general conversation.

"The secret to successful decorating of a good chocolate cake is to think about the reason you are making it and the person you are making it for."

"I don't understand."

"You will. Now the purpose of this cake is to say a kind farewell to a precious friend who is about to leave us."

"That doesn't sound a very happy event; I don't think I want to hear any more, thank you."

"Well, it isn't a happy occasion, I admit, but we can't pretend things are other than they are. This cake will be a memory and, without memories, there could be no reunions between parted friends. We call such things Friendship Cakes."

As, in his dream, Imp thought over what Moon said, he realised that the kitchen was full of people, or maybe it was simply their spirits listening in and approving. There were Earth, Sun, planets, moons, many that he knew and some he did not but, to him, they were all his family.

☽ ☺ ☾

Waking rather earlier than usual, Imp recalled his second dream as if he had not been asleep at all. The earlier one was less clear but somehow he knew that it was very important to him.

He lay back, staring unseeing at his bedroom ceiling. As he did so, the creamy white room seemed to change colour, turning grassy green.

In an instant he re-entered his dream, his mind ran through its whole course: the bright day, the sense of energy all about him, the half-seen figures at their games. He struggled to recall the conversation he had with his unknown companion. – Something about the game of Bowls. – In what way was that important?

Whose voice had spoken to him? To understand, this he had to know.

Suddenly he did know and everything fell into place as he lay there feeling shocked, saddened and oddly excited.

Sun had painted one of her most brilliant ever dawn skies. The sort of sky which no-one who had just seen it on a painter's canvas would believe:

"I like the scene and the people; such a pity that the artist has no idea how to paint skies; that's just ridiculous."

Moon was rolling about in his kitchen, singing softly to himself and making a second breakfast, or supper according to how you wish to look at it. He was also happily doing a little baking. He really is a very good cook.

The room was full of wonderful cooking smells, which this morning were a thrilling mix of toast, bacon, sausages, coffee and, of course, baking. All delicious things that would make anyone want to sit down and spend the rest of the day in that warm, cheerful place.

He was just about to call out that second breakfast, or supper (according to how you looked at life) was ready when Imp appeared, looking rather puzzled and unhappy. Being engrossed in cookery, Moon might not have noticed this but Imp's refusal of a cooked meal and his request for *"Just a piece of toast please"* so shocked Moon that he stopped doing cooking and baking things, sat Imp down and asked what his problem was.

"I'm sorry Moon but I can't tell you yet. I've had a shock. I'll talk to you about it later when my thoughts are clearer."

And that was all Moon could get out of his friend for the time being.

Later, they had a visit from Sun, who was sneaking off for a light lunch with her friends while Earth's sky was covered in thick grey cloud to conceal her absence from trouble-making know-alls.

It was Sun's turn to ask Imp why he was so quiet (actually Sun called it "grumpy" which was unlikely to make Imp feel any better, but that is Sun for you. – Direct!)

This time Imp made no reply at all which, for no obvious reason set Sun laughing so much that she accidentally set light to Moon's last remaining suit of pyjamas which, along with the rest of his creamy coloured laundry had been drying over the cooker. Far from being upset, Moon also burst into laughter and rolled around his kitchen waving the blazing garment around his head – well it takes all sorts to make the Universe!

Imp viewed these goings on with sad tolerance. When his friends had finished their laughing bout, he said:

"I'm sorry to spoil your fun and the pleasure you gain from burning your clothing. I'm sorrier still that my obvious unhappiness is such a source of childish amusement to you both.

I hope what I'm about to say will enable you to see how inappropriate your jollity is and that you will regret your lack of consideration."

This was a characteristically pompous speech from Imp to which the unsympathetic Sun replied:

"Do get off your high horse, Imp. If you have something miserable to say, say it; then we can all have our lunch. I'm starving."

And after Moon had said much the same to Imp and so squashed all hope of him receiving any sympathy rather than hilarity, Imp had no option but to soldier on with his tale which he tried to do, continuing in his most pompous fashion:

"My friends, I thank you both for your concern. The fact is that last night I had dream-sent messages foretelling of changes to my life and the sad loss of dear colleagues…"

Here Sun rudely interrupted Imp's speech before he could take it any further. A good thing too, otherwise we were all likely to fall asleep before Imp got to the heart of his problem.

"Look here, Imp, dreams are all very well but we don't need to hear about them now. The fact is we know perfectly well that your father invited you home after you proved that you've matured out of your silly ways (well, almost) and, more important, into a good Bowls player.

We also know he wanted you to say your goodbyes to us in a kindly fashion so that we all remain on the best of terms.

For my part (and I speak for Moon here as well) I shall miss you and hope you return to stay with us often in the years to come.

Now you can say your piece but make it short as we have a lot of eating to catch up on."

To this Imp replied nothing but Moon said something that sounded like *"Hear. Hear"* although, as it was spoken through a mouthful of toast and butter, it might as well have been *"Dear. Dear."*

At which Imp sat down and silently set about his delayed breakfast, which, incidentally, was not limited to the mere piece of toast he had first requested.

When the meal was over (so far as any meal with Moon is ever truly over) and Sun was preparing a few sandwiches and cakes to go with mid-morning tea, Imp gathered the courage to speak again:

"But I don't understand how you both knew all this without my telling either of you".

"The answer to that, dear old Imp" said Sun "is: you shouldn't talk in your sleep.

As to your second dream, that was telling you we already knew you were leaving; that there was nothing for you to worry about. The hard part of saying goodbye was taken out of your hands.

I think you can say that you are looked after by a kindly power and I, for one, am glad to know it."

It was only then that Imp noticed through an open door a huge chocolate cake on the top shelf of one of Moon's cupboards. It looked exactly like the Friendship Cake that Moon had been making in his dream, only far larger.

News travels very fast in the celestial world. Quite how this happens is one of those wonderful miracles that would stop being wonderful as soon as it was "explained" by over-clever scientists determined on researching everything to destruction and leaving no mysteries for the rest of us to marvel at and enjoy.

So, it was inevitable that the whole Solar System (and more) would know that Imp was returning to his family even before Sun, Moon or Imp had the chance to tell anybody the news.

When they heard of it most were quick to express their regret and wish him well. A few of the more selfish moons and a couple of planets (well, as you ask, it was the two touchy ones; Mars and Pluto) were annoyed that they hadn't been told before the whole Universe got hold of it. But even they soon got over their irritation when they thought about the inevitable going away feast.

As we have seen, Imp was well liked. He was constantly having to promise he would return often to spend time with his friends and share any number of meals with them. But what everyone wanted most was his assurance that he would be back to play their favourite game. Imp hoped he would but wasn't yet sure. He could say only that the future was uncertain.

This uncertainty was partly Imp's own making. He found it hard to fix a date for his going, preferring to avoid the issue for as long as possible. But, as he was troubled by repetitions of the dream that summoned him home, he settled on a day, some months ahead, and told his friends when he would be leaving them.

At once the dream ceased.

As one might expect, the time before Imp's departure was filled with sociable meals, some widely attended feasts and numerous Bowls matches. This was largely Moon's doing with a good deal of help from Sun.

Gentle Earth was usually asleep when anything important (like Imp's farewell feast) was being planned. But she woke from time to time to cast a kindly and approving smile on all about her and check if Moon had made another disappearance. Happily, he had not.

This period, full of cheer mixed with a little sorrow, passed all too quickly for the Friends. It is ever the case that happy days speed gaily past and, by contrast, difficult periods hang around, long outstaying their welcome. If they are lucky enough to enjoy a welcome at all.

When the day came for Imp to leave, he awoke early but got up rather late, having been reluctant to leave, perhaps for the last time, the protective comfort of his bed and a room that was now so very familiar to him. He had done his packing the night before, so as to leave as much as possible of this last day free to spend with Moon.

After the inevitable series of snacks before breakfast and the meal itself (with every imaginable breakfast dish on offer), Imp sailed off together with Moon to say goodbye to as many of his friends as possible and, incidentally, receive a number of unexpected and touching parting gifts.

These were mostly related, of course, to Bowls. They included protective gloves from Earth, a bright red helmet from Mars, a handsomely bound volume of Bowls Rules (all one page of it) which had been sent via messenger from far off Pluto and a large number of firelighters and fire extinguishers.

Returning from their farewell tour, they joined Sun for a good solid lunch followed by a short nap and afternoon tea.

It was time to leave; Moon embraced his friend and Sun slapped Imp on the back in her usual hearty fashion (and helped him upright afterwards). They all stood silently together beside the famous Bowls Green, each with their own happy memories of the place.

"Well, Imp, we are all sorry to see you leave" said Moon *"but it will be a relief not to have to cook so many meals in future and after my night work I look forward to quieter mornings without your cheeky backchat…".*

"And for my part" said Sun, butting in, *"not having to apologise to all the poor unfortunates for your practical jokery is going to make my life much easier, although of course, I shall miss you too."*

Not in the least fooled by his friends' apparent rudeness – which is considered to be the proper form for any parting speech between friends in the Universe – Imp answered in best pompous form:

"My dear and annoying friends, I can assure you it is my heartiest wish to be as far away from you as possible and in the shortest time. Half-starved as I have been, I long for a proper and filling meal of some better quality than I've had the misfortune to eat since meeting you.

Of course I shall miss you both terribly, indeed more than I can say."

At which Moon presented Imp and Sun with a large slice of his Friendship Cake to eat or keep as they might choose:

"May your journey be easy, your fortune for ever kind to you and may your memories of us all remain as clear as they are this day just as we shall remember you. We shall expect your return before long and hope for it every day."

Sun left them both then, thinking in her kindly way that this was best.

Moon and Imp stood silently by the Green, each rather sadly lost in their memories. Suddenly, as if planned for the moment, a Bowls match began. Turmoil was instant with the usual laughter and shrieking, then a great burst of flame. Sun had joined the players and promptly set light to the grass again.

That broke the sorrowful mood. Imp grinned at Moon: *"Wish I could stay!"*

But of course he could not. So Imp departed, slowly fading at first, then quite suddenly vanishing as is the magical way of imps setting out on their journeys.

Moon stood for some time watching the match, then sailed gently back to his home.

Taking up a newly painted portrait of Imp (done of course and given to him by Sun), Moon hung the picture on his kitchen wall next to a portrait of Earth and the much travelled one of smiling Sun.

Having made for himself a pot of tea and, by force of habit, a few pieces of buttered toast, Moon sat back in his rocking chair and silently saluted the three pictures; something he was to do a great may times again in the future.

In case you think he was in for a lonely time, I should mention that Moon was not given long to reflect on the past. Within a few minutes, Sun burst in to regale him with a story about how she had just set light to Mars and repeat an edited version of all that Mars had to say about it.

They both laughed, proving yet again that games are good for everyone whether watcher or player. They sat down to enjoy a modest supper together; well they thought it modest. Afterwards they spoke of Imp and his funny ways, both missing him and finding comfort in their talk together.

What was Earth doing all this time? Sleeping – of course, her kindly dreams reaching far away to Imp's home and the welcome that was being prepared there.

Later, when Sun had left, Moon went into his circular bedroom to get ready for the night's work.

There in the middle of the bedroom floor was a large round parcel with a bright red label.

"For my Great Friend Moon, to use on his travels with the hope that it will serve well, hold sufficient and bring happy memories."

For a moment Moon wondered if this parcel, so obviously from his young friend, might contain an exploding chocolate cake or another rocket but in his heart he already knew what it was.

The large, round, creamy coloured case was simply beautiful. Inside it had round compartments and round containers to carry all the food in his larder, round space enough for all his holiday needs and room to spare for a travelling imp.

He sat down, carefully holding his wonderful gift and let memories run gently through his mind.

As to Imp's return to his family, they were naturally pleased to see him and now very proud of their confident, well-mannered offspring. But he could never awaken their interest in any of his adventures. So far as they were concerned, adolescents may do as they wish on the sole condition they keep it all to themselves.

Does Imp return to see his friends? Of course he does - often. You can't keep a good Bowls player down.

Summer afternoon

**Dreams speak of what has been
and yet shape our future.**

The sun had long gone, replaced by a solid grey sky that threatened rain. The morning's warm, kindly breeze had become a brisk, chilly, late afternoon wind which was doing its best to wake her.

She struggled to stay with her dream as we all do when, in half sleeping state, we cling to some happier world.

Gradually the cold, a little hunger from a missed lunch and ever louder voices nearby, forced her to full wakefulness and, with it, much of her dream vanished leaving only vague memories and a sense of great loss.

She stood, very carefully, as if any sudden move would damage something precious and fragile.

Looking down at the crushed orchard grass and thinking what an amazing amount one may dream in a short time, she wished there was something, anything, to touch and hold and prove to herself that … well, prove what? She was unsure.

A bright flash caught her attention.

The creamy coloured disc lay on an area of close-cropped grass a short distance away. In spite of the overcast sky, it shone brightly as if its light came from inside.

Surely it hadn't been there earlier? Even that short grass seemed to have appeared since she fell asleep.

The thought crossed her mind that, whatever this shining thing was, it wanted to call attention to itself, like a smiling friend beckoning to her.

She stepped lightly across to the neat little lawn, which might have been mown especially for this occasion. Kneeling and picking it up, she looked curiously at the bright little jewel with at first no idea what lay in her hand.

It was surprisingly, and comfortingly, heavy and perfectly circular with two equally round holes near its centre and curiously wavy red stripes on both sides.

It looked like a button; the type one might find on pyjamas but rather too small; a sort of token button.

Whether the little token had some power of its own or if it was just chance, memories of her dreams in the last few hours suddenly flooded into her mind, clear, complete and so welcome.

"That reminds me, I'll support a campaign to have Pluto reinstated." The outspoken thought came without her knowing why or quite what the words meant, only that this was something she had to do.

Her pleasant thoughts ran on for a little longer, happily following threads of memory, like tributaries of a river, wherever they chose to take her, until:

"You've wasted a whole afternoon hiding yourself away. I bet you were sleeping most of it! Dreaming about some stupid thing as ever, I suppose.

And what have you got there? Put it down whatever it is, we don't need any more of your rubbish at home."

And so on. First one of the family, then another, each having their ill-tempered say and she heard it all in silence, her thoughts far away, recovering and storing precious memories she would keep and guard for the rest of her life, just as she was to keep and revere her creamy button token.

"But I haven't wasted it at all" she thought *"and something, somebody, has given me a lot of ideas that I shall use one day."*

And so on. Which of course she has.

9 781739 879112